Hands of Grace

Books by Brenda S. Anderson

THE POTTER'S HOUSE BOOKS (TWO)

Hands of Grace
Song of Mercy (Coming July 2020)
Walk of Faith (Coming December 2020)

THE MOSAIC COLLECTION

A Beautiful Mess

THE POTTER'S HOUSE BOOKS

Long Way Home
Place Called Home
Home Another Way

WHERE THE HEART IS SERIES

Risking Love
Capturing Beauty
Planting Hope

COMING HOME SERIES

Pieces of Granite
Chain of Mercy
Memory Box Secrets
Hungry for Home
Coming Home – A Short Story

Potter's House

THE POTTER'S HOUSE BOOKS (TWO), BOOK 4

Hands of Grace

A NOVELLA

VIVANTPRESS

Minneapolis, Minnesota

Vivant Press
Hands of Grace
Copyright © 2020
Brenda S. Anderson

ISBN-13: 978-1-951664-01-5

This novel is a work of fiction. Names, characters, places, and incidents either are the product of the author's imagination or are used fictitiously. Any resemblance to actual events, locales, organizations, or persons living or dead is entirely coincidental and beyond the intent of either the author or the publisher.

Cover Design by Marion Ueckermann
Cover Photos from Deposit Photos

Printed in the United States of America

20 21 22 23 24 25 26   7 6 5 4 3 2 1

Note from the Author

The 24 books that form **The Potter's House Books Series (Two)** are linked by the theme of Hope, Redemption, and Second Chances. They are all stand-alone books and can be read in any order. Books will become progressively available from January 7, 2020.

Visit **www.PottersHouseBooks.com** for updates on the latest releases.

To caregivers around the world ~

You demonstrate what Hands of Grace really means as you have one of the most difficult, often thankless jobs out there. Know that you are seen, that you are loved, and you are greatly appreciated!

"Ultimately, grace can never be earned.

Like all gifts it can only be received,

requiring that I simply open my hands and trust."

— Mark Yaconelli, **The Gift of Hard Things** —

Chapter One

What was the appropriate outfit to wear for getting engaged? At least, her boyfriend had hinted at proposing.

Rita Dunlap stared into her too-small closet and sorted through her meager offerings. If this was just any guy, she'd choose her little black dress that she'd worn for many special occasions, but Robert was different.

A heart surgeon deserved to see her in something new. Something special. But her budget prohibited her from purchasing anything new, and her caregiving duties didn't allow her time to rummage through the racks at the used-clothing store.

She slid each hanger to one side as she rummaged through them. There! On the end, her indigo sheath fell forward. Close to black, but not quite. She removed it from the closet and hurried to the bathroom. The mirror in her momma's home seemed to be warped with age, but it sufficed for right now.

She held the dress below her chin—it brought out the blue in her eyes and emphasized the red underlayers in her otherwise coffee-colored hair. Its hourglass shape would add dimension to her too-straight figure.

Robert would love it on her. She hoped.

She carried the dress back to her bedroom and laid it on the bed.

Nope. No doubting. Wasn't that what her best friend would tell her? Before Rita had messed up her life, Lissa had been a deep well of wise advice that Rita had sloughed off as Puritan.

It took losing everything for her to realize that Lissa had been right.

Which was why she'd been picky about who she dated, but even she hadn't anticipated attracting a Christian doctor.

God is good.

She glanced at her bed stand clock. Only half an hour until he arrived, and she had so much to do yet, including giving her momma the news that she'd be gone tonight, and a caregiver would be staying with her. Thanks to Robert, who footed the bill.

Yes, he was a good man.

Once she and Robert married, Rita wouldn't have to worry about too-few clothes selections, warped mirrors, empty bank accounts. Soon, all her problems, all her worries would vanish faster than her savings had when she'd been fired from her last job.

She hurried to the living room where Momma sat in her favorite rocking chair, her legs lifted on the rocking ottoman. All day long she sat watching the old-time-TV channel. *Andy Griffith* followed by *Father Knows Best* and then *Leave it to Beaver* and *Gilligan's Island*. Right now, *Green Acres* was on.

Approaching her mother, the familiar tension weighted her arms. When would she overcome that? This was her mother, for Pete's sake. She smoothed her hands at her side, forced a smile, and stood beside her momma's chair. "How is your show?"

"Shhh." Momma aimed the remote at the television, raising the volume. "I don't think I've seen this one before."

Rita bit her tongue, stopping the words that would remind Momma she'd watched this very episode a week or two ago, and probably not long before then. "Is it a good one?"

"Mm hmm."

"I'm going out tonight. Joni Becker's coming to stay with you."

"Johnnie?" Momma sat up straight. "He's coming here?" She pushed out of her rocker. "Then I have to get ready. I can't have him seeing me like this."

"Of course not." Why bother explaining who Joni was when her mother would forget the next minute? "Do you need help getting dressed?"

"I'm perfectly capable of dressing myself." Momma toddled off to her bedroom.

And Rita shook her head. She couldn't wait to see what outfit her mother dressed in today. They might be garish, but the independence of choosing clothes and dressing herself was far more important than wearing something stylish. Momma's younger, stylish self would be horrified.

For Rita, it was amusing. Finding sources of laughter was so important with this nasty disease.

She hurried back into her room, finished her hair and makeup, then put on her dress. Going sleeveless wasn't the brightest idea as Minnesota's September evening air was cooling drastically already, so she chose a light blue shawl to go over it. She checked herself in the bathroom mirror again.

Not bad, if she did say so herself. She couldn't wait to see Robert's expression, which should happen soon. He was always appreciative of the work she put into making herself beautiful for him.

She retrieved her two-inch-heeled pumps from her closet and

checked the clock. She had five minutes to spare—well, more like ten or fifteen. Timeliness wasn't one of his positive traits, but no one was perfect, right?

Someone knocked on the door, and her heart did a little tango. Was he here already? Or was it Joni?

She hurried to the front door, her mother puttering from the bedroom behind her.

"Is it Johnnie?" Mother asked. "I'm all ready for him."

"Joni might be here to watch movies with you." Rita resisted turning around to see how her momma was dressed. "She loves rom coms."

"So, he's taking me out to the movies? How lovely!"

Rita sighed, digging her fingers into her palms as she stopped at the front door. She counted to ten, slowly uncurling her fingers, and then drew on a smile for whoever had knocked.

Hopefully, Robert.

She opened the door and disappointment tugged down her shoulders. "Hi Joni, thanks for coming."

The college-aged woman bopped into the house. "Happy to be here. Hi Gladys. How's it going? Love your outfit."

"Johnnie's taking me to the movies tonight."

Rita closed the door, turned toward her mom, and had to stifle her laugh. Momma sure loved her bright colors. From sock to hat, she was adorned with vibrant patterns, all of which clashed. Then there was the garish makeup and failed attempt at a bun.

But if Momma thought she was beautiful, Rita would leave it at that.

"Is that so?" Joni took Momma's arm and led her to the couch. "Then how about you and I sit and watch something while we wait?" She dug into the canvas bag she always brought with her that seemed as bottomless as Mary Poppins' carpet bag. "*That Touch of Mink* with Cary Grant and Doris Day?"

Momma drew in a quick breath and clapped her hands. "My favorite."

"I knew it." Joni winked at Rita, telling her she was free to go. Momma would be too occupied by the movie to realize Rita was leaving.

She found her clutch, wrapped the shawl over her shoulders, snuck out the side door, and walked to the front of the house to wait for Robert.

Five minutes she stood there.

Six.

Seven.

"Bad Case of Loving You" started playing on her phone. Robert's ringtone. She dug the phone from her clutch and answered. "Hey there. I'm ready for you."

"About that." His slight Southern drawl was followed by a deep sigh.

She knew what that meant. Tonight was off. "Called into surgery?" She resisted rubbing her hand over her nose.

"Just got out, which means I have to head straight to the restaurant. Do you mind driving yourself?"

"We're still on for tonight?"

"Darlin', we have big plans. No way am I going to miss. But I have reservations, and if I stop to pick you up, we'll be late, and they'll give our table to someone else. Can I meet you there?"

"Of course," she said with as much of a positive inflection she could muster. Driving herself in her ancient Chevy wasn't nearly as romantic as being picked up in Robert's Tesla. "I should get there in twenty minutes."

"That's why I love you, darlin'. I'll see you soon, and make sure that finger is ready for some new jewelry."

"I can't wait." A warm tingle coursed through her body as she stared down at her empty ring finger. Her nails were lacquered with a shiny red polish, but weren't nearly as nice as if she'd had a professional manicure. Not in her money or time budget. But her lack of wearing designer clothing never fazed Robert. He loved her just as she was.

She dug her car key out of her purse and hurried to her coupe parked on the slab of crumbling concrete adjacent to the alley in back of the home. With some jiggling, she got the rusty door to unlock, then she sank into her low-to-the-ground coupe, trying unsuccessfully to sit with grace. Coupes were not made for women wearing dresses.

Before inserting the key into the ignition, she prayed the engine would turn over. It had been fussy lately. Robert had told her not to worry, that soon her problems would be taken care of. Oh, she hoped so.

She stuck the key into the ignition and, closing her eyes, turned the key. The engine putted and sputtered. The car shook and roared to life, wanting to shoot into the alley. Then the engine mellowed and calmed to as normal as it would get. Normal enough to venture out onto the roads. *Thank you, God.* Now to make it the ten miles to the other side of Rochester without breaking down.

Fifteen minutes later, she chugged into the parking lot of MacMillan's on the Lake, the priciest restaurant in the area. She bypassed the valet who looked relieved when she didn't slow, and parked beneath a lamp.

Now to get out of the car gracefully. Keeping her knees together, she started pushing up.

"May I help you?" a deep voice with a slight Southern lilt

asked, and her heart did that little jig.

She looked up into Robert's impossibly natural caramel eyes and, as always, they melted her into a puddle. She gave him her hand, and he deftly assisted her from her beater then closed the door behind her.

"I'm so sorry I couldn't pick you up." He offered his elbow, which she gratefully accepted, and they walked toward the building. "As soon as I have a moment, you and I are going car shopping. The thought of you being stranded on the freeway terrifies me."

"But I can't afford—"

"It will be my gift."

"That's too much."

He stopped and cupped her chin, looking her in the eye. "Darlin', nothing is too much for you."

Her mouth went dry as he gave her a soft kiss.

Oh my.

Her entire body overheated and turned to mush. A few years back she would have asked him to skip the meal and go directly to his home or a hotel, but she was no longer that woman whose morals were looser than a sweater three times her size.

Robert respected that. Another thing to love about him.

She shivered, thinking of the woman she used to be.

He wrapped his arm around her waist, drawing her closer as they walked, his woody cologne drifting subtly her way.

With him, she felt cherished, not used like every other man in her adult life had treated her.

He escorted her into the building, and the maître d' showed them to their table. Apropos to the establishment's name, the restaurant sat on the edge of a lake and the interior was arranged so that each table had a water view. Absolutely beautiful. He hadn't taken her here before. Truthfully, they never went to the same place twice.

She sat in a high-backed, cushy booth with Robert across from her. It almost felt as if they had their own private room. This was a perfect spot to get engaged.

"Comfortable?" He extended his arm across the table, and she took his hand.

"Very. This place is . . . "

"Breathtaking." His gaze didn't waver from her.

She blushed, her voice stolen.

He made it worse by smiling and winking.

Heaven help her, she'd do anything for this man, so she looked away and picked up the hard-backed menu with one single page between its covers. No prices were shown beside the four entrees offered, all promising seasonal foods sourced from local farmers. Her gaze landed on the mushroom linguine with lemon. Sounded delectable.

"Their prime rib is unbeatable," Robert said, laying down his menu. "But I'm assuming you're going with the linguine."

How did he always know? Was she that predictable? "Maybe I'll shake things up and go with the New York strip."

He grinned. "Maybe you should."

"I'll do just that." She closed her menu and set it aside.

But when the waiter took their order, "Mushroom linguine" spilled from her lips. So what if she was predictable? Robert loved her anyway.

They talked about his surgery that afternoon, as much as he could without violating HIPAA laws. She shared how, on her daily walk with her mother, Momma had become terrified when she didn't recognize the neighborhood or even her home of thirty-plus years. Over the meal, he promised again that he would move Momma in with them once they were married, and would hire Joni on full time. Over dessert, Rita couldn't concentrate on what they talked about—all she wanted was to see the ring.

The *Doctor Who* theme rang out, and Robert grimaced as he pulled the phone from his pocket. "I told you, I'm not on call tonight." His brows slowly drew together, and the sides of his lips drooped downward.

No. They couldn't ruin her perfect evening.

"Fine. I'll be in." He jabbed at his phone and shoved it into his interior jacket pocket.

"Another emergency?" She wanted to be sympathetic, really, she did, but her own heart was going to require surgery if she didn't get proposed to soon.

"You'd think that in a town renowned for the Mayo Clinic, they'd have a wealth of surgeons to choose from."

"But you're the best."

He shook his head and reached across the table. "I'm so sorry, Rita."

She laid her hands in his. "This is your life. You save people. How can I be angry about that?"

"Right, but . . . " He reached into his jacket pocket and pulled out a white jewelry box.

She gasped.

He held the small box in his palm without opening it. "I'm not proposing now. I can't. The night needs to be special, like this one should have been, but know, my darlin' Rita, it's coming."

"I know," eked from her lips.

He waved over the waiter and paid for the meal in cash, as he always did, then got up and offered his hand to her. "Call me when you get home. I need to know you arrive safely."

"I will."

"And make sure Joni sends her bill to me."

That wasn't a problem. No way could Rita pay for the personal care assistant.

They walked from the restaurant and arrived at her car. Before helping her in, he gave her a kiss that had her shrugging off her shawl.

"Soon, darlin'." He cupped her cheek with a hand. "Soon, you will be Mrs. Smithson. That's a promise." He gripped her hand as she lowered into her car.

And she held her breath as he gently closed the rattily door. No, he hadn't officially proposed, but he'd made a promise. That was good enough to send her floating up to the clouds. Someday soon, she would be Mrs. Robert—

Something pounded on her car door. Startled, she looked out the window. Robert? She cranked it down.

"Darlin', there's something else I completely forgot about. Being with you clatters my brain and I can't think of anything else." He held up a thick padded envelope. "I was supposed to pick up my sister's gift tonight. I have an appointment with the artist, and now I can't make it. I hate asking this of you, but I really need it by tomorrow for her birthday. Would you mind?"

Anything to help her be accepted by his sister and family. They hadn't been happy to meet her that one time. No doubt, she wasn't good enough for their brother and son. "Of course."

He puffed out a breath. "Thank you, thank you." He offered her the thick envelope. "This'll pay for the vase. You can pick it up here." He scribbled on another piece of paper and handed it to her. "Ask for Corina, say you're picking up the vase for Marion."

She repeated the instructions in her mind. "Got it."

"Have I said how much I love you?" He leaned down and gave her a too-quick kiss. "Sorry. Gotta go. There are lives on the line." And then he was off, jogging toward his Tesla.

Okay, then. She remained there, watching him peel away to save some life. The least she could do was help him preserve his relationship with his sister.

She put the key in the ignition and turned. The engine sputtered and quit. She tried again. It chugged a bit longer. And quit.

She pounded the steering wheel. "You old hunk of junk!" she grunted out, but wanted to say something far less family friendly. "Okay, God. I don't know if miracles involve starting cars, but I'm asking for a miracle. Please."

As she whispered, "Amen," she tried the key one more time. The engine wheezed, the car rattled, and then the engine finally took hold. "Thank you, Lord," she whispered, letting the engine warm up as she put the artist's address into her phone app. Not too far from here. Fifteen, twenty minutes max. Then she'd hurry home and send off Joni to save Robert the PCA expense.

She put the car in gear and coaxed it down the road and onto the freeway. Twenty minutes later, she arrived at the destination. An unassuming Cape Cod home in a neighborhood that likely housed families. There was no guarantee her junker would start again if she turned it off, so she left it running as she hurried up the steps to the house, the cash-filled envelope in hand. She rang the doorbell and waited.

A fifty-something-ish man answered the door.

"Is there a Corina here?"

"Yeah there is. Come on in."

"Uh, my car's running. I can't stay long."

"Not a problem. Come inside. I'll get Corina. She's quick."

21

Something niggled at Rita, told her to remain outside, but Robert wouldn't send her someplace that wasn't safe, would he?

Still. She glanced back at her car, then inside the house that looked like any other home she'd been in, and stepped inside.

The man closed the door behind her. "Be right back with Corina."

"Okay."

He hurried down a hallway, disappearing from her sight. She stayed close to the door, one hand clutching the envelope, another the doorknob.

A few seconds later, the man reappeared with a woman, who could have been thirty or fifty, carrying a box. The tall, toned woman sure didn't strike Rita as artist, more like a boxer. But what does an artist look like anyway?

"You're looking for Corina?" the woman asked. "Someone else was supposed to meet me."

"He wasn't able to make it. He was called into surgery."

A single brow shot up on the woman's face. "Surgery, huh?"

"Yeah." Rita dragged the word out into three syllables and tried turning the doorknob. It wouldn't budge. Gulping, she backed closer to the wall. "Robert gave me money for it." She held out the envelope. Maybe this would buy her way out.

"So, he did." The woman took the envelope and looked inside, then handed over the box.

"Thanks." She turned toward the door. "I'll just leave—"

The man stepped in front of her, his palm flat against the door. She backed up, bumping into something.

She whirled around.

Make that some*one*.

Somehow the woman who'd accepted the cash had snuck behind Rita, hemming her in. Then both the man and woman shoved badges in front of her eyes. They were police officers?

"Ms. Dunlap, we'd like you to come down to the station and chat with us." The male officer smiled as if trying to be friendly, but she saw accusation in his eyes.

What? Why? "I . . . I don't understand." And how did they know her name? "Am I under arrest?" She hugged herself, trying to calm the shakes.

"Not right now." The woman put her hands on her hips, pulling back her blazer, showcasing a gun.

Rita gulped. "Then I need to go home. My momma needs me."

"Ms. Dunlap." The man mimicked the female cop's stance. "You can come with us voluntarily, or involuntarily."

"But I've done nothing wrong. I just came to buy a vase for my boyfriend."

He smirked. "That's what they all say."

Chapter Two

*I*n a fog, she was transported to the police station then locked away in a room that would fit well in an insane asylum. White walls, a table, and a couple of chairs. She sat down and the female officer sat across from her, laying a folder on the table. The other officer remained by the door.

"Ms. Dunlap." The woman began.

"What's your name again? I need to know who I'm talking to."

"I'm Officer Carol McCain. That's my partner, Detective Cramer." She folded her hands on the table. "You've gotten yourself into trouble, Ms. Dunlap, and we'd like to help you out. How did you get involved with William Flynn?"

"Who's William Flynn?"

Officer McCain shoved a photo of a man in front of her. "Recognize this man?"

Rita looked down at the photo and her heart ramped up speed. It was Robert, or his twin, but with longish, dirty blond hair instead of the above-the-ears brunette cut. Instead of being clean shaven, this man wore a scruffy beard and mustache. She shook her head and shoved back the photo. "Robert has short dark hair and no beard."

"Ah, like this?" The woman slid a different photo across the table. A mugshot of *her* Robert. Maybe a little bit younger, but it was him. Or his twin. He had to have a twin, because her Robert wouldn't do this to her.

"Why were you purchasing drugs for William? Money problems?"

Drugs? William? What were they talking about? It added together like lipstick and mud.

Another picture of Robert was shoved in front of her. A more recent mugshot. It couldn't be him. It just couldn't be.

Her breaths came in quick waves as she stared at the pictures strewn on the table.

"Caring for your mother has got to be a strain," the officer said as if trying to sympathize.

Oh, no! Momma! How could she have forgotten?

"Please, I have to get home to my momma." She pushed away from the table and stood. "She has dementia and is at home with a caregiver who has to leave by eleven. I need to get home to care for her. She can't be alone. She needs me." *She needs me.* Rita fell back on the chair, and her tears could no longer be restrained. They rolled down her cheeks, down her chin, and dripped onto her dress, making ugly blotches on the material.

"Cooperate with us, and we'll get you home in plenty of time."

"I've done nothing wrong. I was just picking up a vase for Robert, for his sister."

"Robert. So that's what he's calling himself nowadays."

"Yes. Doctor Robert Smithson. He's a heart surgeon at the Mayo. Check it out." Because that man in the photos couldn't be her Robert. He just couldn't be.

"Another Bob Smith." Detective Cramer chuckled behind her. "You'd think he'd be more creative than that by now."

"You'd think." The woman smirked. "And the doctor angle always gets the gullible girls."

"I'm not . . . " She cut herself off and raised her chin. She wasn't going to whine to them. Sure, in the past she'd fallen for boyfriends and their schemes, but Robert was different.

Officer McCain bore her gaze into Rita. "You were picking up a vase?"

"Yes. We'd just come from MacMillan's, and he was called into surgery. He asked me to pick up the vase for him."

"The vase filled with oxycodone?"

"No! Just a vase. A gift for his sister."

"His sister. Have you met her?"

"Yes. Once."

"Is this her?" The officer slid a different photo over to Rita. A rosy-cheeked blonde who looked to be about sixteen years old.

A youngish version of Robert's younger sister, Marion.

Sucking on her lower lip, Rita nodded as the truth smacked her heart: Robert had played her, and she'd fallen for him without blinking an eye.

She thought she'd done everything right this time. Gotten involved with a single man. A doctor. One who sat in church with her. Yes, she'd made mistakes with men in the past, tried to purchase their love, but Robert had been different. He wouldn't have involved her in drug trafficking. He just wouldn't.

She wiped her eyes and sniffled. "I met her at Robert's apartment. I had supper with them and Robert's dad. They were all—"

"Robert's dad?" A dark look flashed across Officer McCain's face as she thumbed through her file. "Is this the man you met?"

A mug shot of a distinguished-looking man with dark hair salted with grey.

"That's him."

Her jaw tensing, Officer McCain stood quickly. "We'll be right back. We need you to stay here. For your safety."

For her safety? In a police station? How wasn't she safe here?

The officers exited the room, leaving her alone with memories of Robert flashing through her brain. Meeting him at the food shelf.

He was volunteering.

She was picking up food.

Yet he'd talked to her, listened to her, laughed with her, treated her like any normal person. When she showed up again the next week, he'd asked her out.

Robert was a good man.

She stared down at the pictures strewn in front of her on the table. Mug shots of Robert. His dad. The photo of Marion wasn't a mugshot, but rather one of those school photos.

That didn't erase the fact that Robert had lied to her. Used her. The proof was right in front of her. How could she have been so gullible again?

A different officer swooped into the room. His face a grim mask. He offered his hand. "ATF Agent Brent Blue. It appears you've stepped into something nasty, Ms. Dunlap. We'd like to offer you protection."

"Protection?"

Officer Blue sat in front of her. "The Flynn family aren't nice people, and you've met the mastermind behind it all. He won't like that."

Her shivers increased, and she stuttered out, "W . . . what are you s . . . saying?"

"We'd like to move you to a safe home for the time being."

Rita shook her head out of unbelief, and to say no. "I can't. My momma needs me."

"She'll come with you."

"She can't. She has dementia, and taking her away from home

will confuse her, and she becomes hysterical. We can't go anywhere."

"You'll be putting both of you in danger."

Rita dipped her head. "I know, but leaving that house will kill my momma. Either way, it's her death sentence."

"Good to have you back, Daniel."

Officer Daniel Winter shook the hand of Howard Cramer, who joined him at the window. Cramer was the officer in charge of this case, and also Daniel's mentor.

"Good to be back."

"Your head's screwed on straight?"

Daniel laughed. "As straight as it'll ever be. But yeah, I'm ready to dive in headfirst."

"Good to hear that, 'cause we got a deep, churning river you'll be taking a swim in." Howard nodded at the two-way mirror, toward the distraught woman at the table.

Daniel had been watching since they brought her in. Young woman, probably in her thirties. Sharply dressed. Dark hair with bright red peeking out from underneath as if she wanted to hide her quirks.

What else was she hiding?

He well understood her conflict about not wanting to be relocated, even temporarily, having watched his grandma struggle for years with dementia.

Oh, he'd like to wring the necks of the Flynn family. Their extended family and cohorts flitted from one big city to the next, preying on the vulnerable, often sucking the naïve into their trade with offers of easy money.

Caring for a parent with dementia possibly meant her funds were limited and she could be easily tempted by the Flynns.

Had William Flynn, aka Dr. Robert Smithson, been grooming Rita Dunlap for his family business? Or was she just another pawn he planned to use then throw away?

"You think she's telling the truth?" He asked Howard, a longtime member of the force, someone whose opinion Daniel respected deeply.

"About not knowing who her boyfriend was?"

Daniel nodded.

"I do. Or she deserves to win an Oscar. We blindsided her with the info, and she was shaken. As you can see, she's still trying to process it."

"Yeah. My thoughts, too." They both stared quietly at the woman, seated alone in the room, probably scared to death. She had reason to be frightened.

"Until proven otherwise, though, she's a suspect."

"Makes sense." He knew too well what happened when you let your guard down. And given her financial troubles, offers of easy money would be difficult to turn down. "What's the status on her *boyfriend*?"

"He's locked up, thanks to an anonymous tip, and his mouth is shut tighter than the cell. We're keeping an eye on the sister in Waukegon, Illinois, where she owns a bakery. Nothing out of the ordinary there—from everything we've gathered so far, she's managed to avoid the family biz. With William locked up and his girlfriend under surveillance, this is our first solid opportunity to get Papa Flynn, and shut down this line of trafficking for good."

Daniel would be praying for that. Before coming in, he'd brushed up on the Flynns, almost making him late for the first part of Rita Dunlap's interrogation. For too long, the Flynn cadre had gotten away with blackmailing physicians and pharmacists, so they had a free flow of prescribed opioids at their disposal. Those addicted were willing to pay dearly for the drugs. The Flynns needed to be stopped, and the best way to do that would be to cut off the ruthless head: Raymond (Papa) Flynn.

Daniel studied the terrified woman in the interrogation room. "Why is a safe house even necessary? If she's telling the truth, she has no knowledge of the drug trade, so her witness is important, but far from a slam dunk."

"Because if she's telling the truth, and she's met that father, anyone who meets him either ends up working for the Flynns or dead."

Oh.

Daniel puffed out a breath. How quickly life could change. One minute you think you're in love, the next minute you're wolf feed.

He dug his hands into his jean pockets. "What's the plan? You can't force her into a safe house, and I understand why she'd refuse." He looked back through the mirror. "She's got a tough gig, caring for her mom."

"First step is to set up some undercover security." Howard propped his hands on his hips. "We located a vacant apartment across the street from her house. We're getting Steinbach and Wallace set up there now, but we want someone closer. On-site."

"How do you plan to do that?"

"Still know how to swing a hammer?"

"Little bit." His dad was a contractor, his mom a retired roofer, and Daniel had flipped houses for years, including this past year's sabbatical from the force. He'd better know a thing or two about wielding a hammer. "I still have my license, I maintain my website, have a great BBB rating, not to brag or anything."

Howard snorted but quickly mellowed. "Good to hear. That'll make your assignment easier to begin right away. The guys did some dumpster diving. Apparently, Ms. Dunlap's mom likes to enter contests. Thanks to the Rochester PD, she just won free handyman services."

"And I'm the handyman."

Howard slapped him on the back. "Yep. Do whatever keeps you busy and on-site. You get to be a one-man show. Who knows, maybe that home channel will start a new show, *Flipping Cops*."

"Don't give 'em any ideas. What about budget? Materials?"

He laughed. "You want a budget?" They looked back through the mirror. "Compound Lumber offered to supply what we need at cost as a thank-you for jailing the arsonist last year. And he's got a 'free' stock we can choose from as well. We want to catch Flynn, so do what you have to do to maintain cover."

"I'll do my best to keep costs in line. And I've got extra materials lying around home as well. May as well put them to good use." And clear out his storage shed in the process. He rubbed his hands together. "The Flynns have been a pain in our country's backside for too long. When do I start?"

"Be ready to show up at her place tomorrow morning. We'll have official-looking documents for you. After this episode, she's gonna be skittish."

"She will be." And she wasn't the only one. The last time he'd done some work for a pretty young woman, she'd done a renovation on his heart before tearing it apart. Problem was that was the second time in the last six years he'd allowed a woman close enough to hurt him. He was wiser now, though. That wouldn't happen again.

"I take it, since she's a suspect, I'm undercover to her as well." Daniel nodded toward the mirror.

"Exactly. Keep it under wraps for now, in case she knows more about the Flynn operation than she's letting on. See what you can learn from her. Even if she is innocent, she might know more about Papa Flynn than she realizes."

"So, keep her safe while I'm snooping around."

"That's it."

"Gotcha." He headed for home to prepare for his assignment: protect Rita Dunlap. He could do that without losing his heart.

Chapter Three

After Officer Blue walked her to the door of her momma's home, he requested permission to check out the yard and neighborhood. She unlocked the door, yet remained outside on the steps. Exhausted. Heartbroken. Terrified. Officer Blue had also assured her that the police would frequently drive past the home to make sure she was safe, but in a drive-by, how could they really tell what was going on inside?

Maybe it was time to get a gun. She shivered just thinking about why that might be necessary.

She knocked on the front door to let Joni know she was home, then let herself in. She'd called Joni before leaving the station, apologized profusely for being late. The young caregiver had gracefully said it wasn't a problem. She and Momma were having a good time watching Cary Grant movies and eating lots of popcorn.

Like they didn't have a care in the world.

Right now, dementia would be a blessing. What she'd give to forget about Robert, er, William, or whoever the jerk was. To think that, once again, she'd fallen for the wrong man and, once again, he'd gotten her to do his dirty work for him.

Why was she so trusting?

Seated on the sofa, Joni welcomed her home, a bright smile on her face. Which faded way too quickly.

"I take it your date didn't go well." Joni set aside the book she held.

Rita snorted. "That's the understatement of the year." She slumped down in her mother's rocker, her gaze quickly darting to the front window. The shades were drawn. Good.

"Care to talk about it?" Joni sat on the edge of the couch, her hands folded in her lap.

Never. Rita shook her head. "It's over. Robert was a snake."

"Oh, no, I'm so sorry." Joni remained on the sofa, her head bowed.

Rita just wanted her to leave so she could go to bed and wake up in the morning to learn that this had been a nightmare, that Robert was who he claimed he was, that she was about to live Cinderella's life.

Ha!

She kicked off her heels and flung them across the floor. They didn't break, which meant they weren't made of glass, and she had no fairy godmother who'd make this better.

"I hate to tell you this."

Rita's head jerked up. There was more?

"Um, payment from Robert never arrived. Usually, he pays a little late, so I wasn't worried, but it never arrived."

Really, God? After the night I've had, now this too? It was time to break out a bag of Pop Rocks. She'd given up the crackly candy a year ago, but maybe it was okay to indulge again. They had always calmed her nerves, while irritating those around her. A year ago, she hadn't cared.

"How much does he owe you?" She braced herself for the answer, but still groaned when Joni named the amount. She couldn't pay it, not if she and Momma wanted to eat this week.

"I'm sorry, I don't have the money right now. Can I please pay

Hands of Grace

in increments?" Once upon a lifetime ago, she'd been a bill collector. Now she understood how it felt being on the other end.

Joni raked her teeth over her lower lip and nodded. "A quarter of it per week? I need to pay tuition by the end of the month."

"Sure." Rita dug into her purse and pulled out the last of her cash for the week. It might not be much to others, but to her it was food for her and Momma. Her mother's meds. Gas. "Here you go. And thank you. Guess I won't be needing you anymore."

And she'd be making another trip to a local food shelf, a place that distributed free food to the poor. Oh, she hated being lumped into that category! But now she'd have to find a different location. She refused to go where she'd met Robert/William.

Joni accepted the cash. "Thank you. And I'm sorry."

Rita shrugged. "Thank you. You've been an amazing caregiver for Momma."

After Joni left, Rita scurried through the home, making certain all the doors and windows were locked and the shades pulled. She kept a nightlight on in the bathroom for her mom, but that was an interior room that wouldn't shine light outside. She also checked the unfinished basement hopper windows. Were they too small for someone to crawl through? Guess it depended upon the size of the intruder.

She shivered.

If only she could afford an alarm system. Maybe she should have gone to the safe house. Momma would have adjusted. Maybe. Probably not. But wasn't alive better than fearful? She imagined Momma in a strange place, freaking out, likely shortening her life. That was no way to live either.

As frightened as she was, staying put was the best for Momma.

At last she went to her bedroom, where she changed into

flannel pajamas without turning on the light—she didn't want anyone to see her from outside. Or maybe she should turn on every light. What was the best thing to do?

She laid down in bed, pulling the covers up over her eyes, but every creak from the old house kept her awake. When the house wasn't groaning, horror scenes played through her mind. She glanced at the window to the right of her bed. A gunman could easily shoot right through it and hit her, so she took her pillows and blankets and spread them on the floor on the side of the bed opposite the window.

She didn't have a bat or anything to protect herself if someone came in. Tomorrow, she'd rectify that.

Tonight, she hoped for sleep and wished for something to mend her shattered heart.

Robert. A sob hiccupped from her throat.

Or was he William?

She clutched a pillow to her chest as grief shuddered through her.

He'd loved her. Had treated her like she was a princess. How could she not have seen his duplicity?

She grabbed the tissue box off her side table and dabbed a wad of tissues at her eyes.

How was she to convince her heart that he'd only been using her, because her heart was still in love with him—or the façade he'd shown to her—and her head wasn't too far behind.

Why was she so easily used? Did she have a sign on her back that read, "Hi, I'm Gullible Rita!"?

She even hiccupped a chuckle with that.

Was she too trusting? Yes. Most definitely. But she also knew how to bounce back up after being shoved down.

Robert had offered her hope that led right into a pit of vipers.

She'd do whatever it took to climb out of that pit, and if that meant helping jail that viper family, that was exactly what she'd do.

Daniel checked in with Officer Steinbach, who was stationed in the apartment across the street from Rita Dunlap's dilapidated rambler. If any place needed a renovation, it was this one. At least he'd keep himself busy during this assignment. Officer Steinbach reported there'd been no unusual activity in or around the house and that Rita and her mom were both home. Patrols reported the same. No doubt, the Flynns were being just as wily about watching for police and were staying hidden for now.

Hopefully, he could outsmart them. Taking down the Flynn family would be a coup for his career and would earn back the respect he'd lost a year ago.

He went out the back door of the apartment and through an alley to his pickup. Winter Handyman Services decals still clung to the doors and the tailgate, and the truck bed was filled with tools of the trade. Remodeling, construction, and repairs he could easily handle; the acting job required of this undercover assignment was a whole lot more difficult.

He drove around the block and parked in front of the home. More weeds than grass grew in the yard. No flowers skirted the house. A towering and aging oak tree needed to be trimmed before a storm heaved branches onto the roof. Not problems that could be solved in a day, but he'd lay the foundation.

With the fake contest credentials in hand, he got out of the truck and strode up to the front door that cried for a new paint job. As did the siding on the entire house. He pressed the doorbell, but heard nothing. He tried knocking instead and listened.

This time, he heard heavy footsteps. The door flung open and a fifty- maybe sixty-year-old woman answered the door, dressed in an outfit that would put Joseph and his multi-colored coat to shame.

Looking at her, his smile came easy. "Is Gladys Dunlap home?" He handed over a business card that read Winter Handyman Services, LLC. At least, that part of his undercover assignment wasn't a lie. During undercover jobs, staying close to the truth always worked best and helped prevent slip-ups.

"That's me." The woman stood straighter and patted her hair.

He couldn't help but grin. The old gal was flirting.

"Momma!" A voice called frantically from somewhere in the house. "What have I told you about opening the door?" The voice neared, and then Rita Dunlap appeared, looking as if she'd been awake all night, with dark shadows circling her eyes and hair that needed a good combing.

Her pink flannel pajamas were rather cute though.

"My date is here." The mother licked her lips and pursed them. "I'll be back before dark. Maybe."

Ms. Dunlap shook her head while putting an arm around her mother's shoulders. "Then shouldn't you finish putting on your makeup, first?"

"Oh, my, yes. Thank you!" The woman shuffled off.

And Ms. Dunlap sighed. "I'm sorry about that." Her gaze seemed to scan the outdoors, landing on his truck, then on him. "I realize this house and yard look like they need it, but if you're here to sell Momma handyman services, the answer is 'no.'" She began to shut the door.

He spread his palm on the door, preventing it from closing. "Actually, your mother won my services." He dug another business card from his pocket and tried handing it to her.

She ignored it. "Likely story." She attempted shutting the door again, pushing harder.

"Ma'am, I'm serious. Your mother entered the Radical House Makeover contest, and she won." Along with his card, he handed her the official-looking document naming Gladys Dunlap as winner.

Ms. Dunlap took the paper and studied it, probably scouring the fine print. Then she glanced up and down the street with wary eyes. "Okay, what's the catch? You come in, do some work, and leave things half done so we have to pay for you to finish?"

No surprise, the woman was skeptical. While that made her acceptance of him more difficult, in the long run it would make his job easier. She wasn't inclined to open the door to anyone.

"No, ma'am, we come—"

"Do not call me ma'am."

He grinned. "Then what should I call you?"

"Rita's fine. I'm Gladys's daughter. She has dementia and can't make decisions like this, so you'll have to deal with me."

"I'm sorry to hear that, about the dementia, that is."

"Yeah. Me, too." She looked down. Clearly, her mom's disease was Ms. Dunlap's—Rita's weak spot, something he'd have to keep in mind. He'd use it now to gain access to her home.

"My grandma had dementia, too. The last years of her life she spent at my folks' place were tough. My mom pretty much had to give up everything to care for her mom."

"What we do for family, right?"

"You're the caregiver, then?"

"Full time, volunteer, which is why we can't afford you. You may as well get back in your pickup and find another sucker."

Okay, that backfired. Time to give it the straightforward approach.

"Ma'am, I mean, Rita." Way to win her over, Slick. "The truth is, your mother won a home makeover and handyman services for the next couple months. I'm going to paint the house. Fix anything that's broken. Clean up the yard."

"All exterior?"

"I can do what's needed inside as well. If it's broken, I'll fix it."

She stepped outside and closed the door behind her. "If you come inside, she'll think you're here on a date. Not kidding."

"I sort of gathered that when she answered the door."

"There's absolutely no cost to us? What about taxes? I know the government has its hands out too when someone wins something."

"Paid for by the contest promoters."

"Really?" Skepticism sunk her voice.

He gestured to the document she clutched in her hands. "You read the fine print. What does it say?"

She sighed, her shoulders heaving with it. "I've learned that when something seems too good to be true, it is. This." She slapped the document in her hands. "Is too good, too convenient."

Wow. He expected her to put up a little fight, but this? He held up his hands as if surrendering. "If you have any questions, doubts, call the number on that page. They'll tell you exactly what I said."

"I wouldn't expect otherwise from scammers."

"What can I tell you that'll convince you I'm legitimate? I'm not leaving, because the company sponsors don't pay me if I don't do the work, and I like to get paid."

"Just not from me." She crossed her arms over her chest.

"Not a penny from you or your mom."

Her jaw shifted back and forth. "Fine. But I need to know

exactly what you plan to do. I want it in writing with your signature on the bottom swearing that I don't owe you a cent."

"If that's what it takes."

She gave a slow, confident nod. "That's what it takes."

"Fine. I'll go call the office, relay your instructions, and have them deliver the form."

"Uh-uh. First, I'm going to make some phone calls. Then we'll talk. Maybe."

"Got it." Shaking his head, he returned to his pickup and relayed the conversation to Howard. "How she got mixed up with the Flynns, I'll never know. The woman's a hound. She senses I'm not being honest and won't give an inch."

"Or maybe when you've been hurt like that, you learn not to budge."

Right. A lesson he'd learned himself when it came to romance.

"Hold a second, Margo says I got a call from Ms. Dunlap on the other line."

Smart woman. He probably seemed like an oily salesman to her. A minute later, Howard came back on the line. "Apparently Miss Dunlap doesn't trust this pseudo-construction worker at her house. I'm gonna go out in person to reassure her. Not that I blame her when she got a look at your ugly mug."

"I know, right?" He scratched at his whiskers he'd intentionally not shaved to help add credibility to his act. "And you'll have a courier deliver some official-looking document for her to sign?"

"On that right now. And then I'm off to convince Ms. Dunlap of your sincerity. Toughest job I've had all month."

"I'll bet. In the meantime, I'll hang out here, keeping an eye on the place."

It was a good twenty minutes before Howard pulled up in his

cruiser behind Daniel's pickup. That was one way to offer believability. Daniel got out of his pickup and chatted with his friend to make it look like Howard was doing an interrogation, before they both walked up to the house.

Howard rang the doorbell.

"I don't think it works," Daniel said. "One more thing to fix."

They waited a few seconds, then tried knocking.

Daniel heard scuffling on the inside. He eyed the curtain in the front window being pulled back, then the door was finally cracked open.

"Detective Cramer." She squeezed through the narrow opening.

Why? What didn't she want them to see? What did she have to hide?

She offered her hand to Cramer. "Thanks for coming by."

"Glad to be of assistance." He gestured to Daniel. "Everything checks out with him. Looks like you are the proud winners of a home makeover and handyman services. Mr. Winter's references check out as well. Customers appear to be pleased with his work."

She seemed to deflate with her sigh. "You don't know what a relief that is." She looked to Daniel. "I'm sorry for not trusting you, but right now I have serious trust issues."

Daniel hiked a shoulder then relaxed. "Always better to check things out thoroughly. I'd rather you be confident that I am who I say I am."

Guilt niggled at him for that. Yes, he was a carpenter, and he would be doing work, but his official job was police officer. He was just one more person lying to her, building up her bank of mistrust. Hopefully, they'd wrap up this case without her learning his real identity. But for now, she was still on their suspect list.

"Is that all you need, Ms. Dunlap?" Howard took a step back.

"That's all. Thank you again. I don't mean to be a bother."

"Your safety is my job. Bother us all you wish." Howard doffed his cap. "Have a good day."

"You too." She sank down on the steps and covered her face with her hands, her head shaking. "My life is surreal right now." She pulled down her hands and looked over at him, patting the crumbling cement step beside her. "Have a seat, show me what you plan to do."

He sat, flipped open a notebook, and gestured to the sides of the crumbling, concrete steps. "Would you like new steps? Railings?"

"Both would be amazing. Momma's having some difficulty walking down the stairs, so railings would be a tremendous help."

"How about a doorbell that works?"

She laughed. "Would love it, but my momma might too."

"So, no doorbell?"

"Yes, to the doorbell. It's just something I have to deal with."

He marked that on his list after steps and railing. "Paint color? You want the same color or something different?"

"Any color?"

"It's your house."

"Well, technically it's my momma's, and she always said she wanted a pale-yellow house with white trim."

"Yellow, it is." He wrote down: Get paint samples. Repair broken trim. Caulk. Then he looked upward. "Do you know how old the roof is?"

"No clue. Momma's lived here for thirty-plus years. I think she replaced it once in that time."

"I'll check it out, see what needs to be done." He jotted down: Replace roof, an assumption made based on the rest of the house's lack of maintenance. "Anything special you want done with the yard?"

"Grass would be wonderful, although weeds are easier to take care of."

He laughed. "Isn't that the truth." He wrote "New grass" in his notes. He'd have to think about whether sod or more black dirt and reseeding was the best route.

"Um, back to the stairs. Would it be possible for you to put in a ramp instead of redoing the steps?"

"Sure. Not a problem."

She actually smiled. "That would be amazing. Momma's not ready for a wheelchair yet, but the time is coming, and I'd like to be prepared."

"Then adding a ramp's a wise move." He stood. "Mind if we do a walk around? See what else needs to be done?"

"Sure." She got up and locked the door. "Momma has difficulty with the deadbolt, so when I lock it, she doesn't wander."

He backed down the sidewalk, slowly appraising the small rambler. The front window had a broken windowpane. He gestured to it with his pen. "I'll replace the glass."

To the left of the house, a large oak branch hovered over the roof, threatening to fall. A good wind could bring it right down. He pointed to the thick branch. "I'll get that down, too."

"Really?"

"It's a radical makeover, that means doing big things."

"Will there be TV cameras too?"

He laughed. "Just before and after pictures."

"You're for real . . ."

"That's what I keep telling you."

She shook her head. "It's just that, in my experience, people don't give me anything without ulterior motives."

"I'm sorry about that." Especially since he was doing that very same thing. He hated this part of his job. A big part of him wondered, when he met Jesus at those pearly gates, would all the lies he'd told, under the guise of his job, flash in front of him? Would Jesus really say, "Well done, good and faithful servant?" Because lies and misdirection were such a big part of his job as an undercover officer, would God excuse that?

"Are you okay?"

He shook his head. "Sorry. Just musing. Take me around the rest of your house."

They followed a decaying sidewalk to the back of the house to a yard the size of a postage stamp. No garage, just a leaning storage shed, by the parking pad, that should be torn down. "Want a new shed?"

"How about a garage?" She grinned. "That would be extreme, right?"

"Well." He scratched the side of his head. "Depends upon city codes. I'll look into it. If this city says, 'It's okay' then you'll get your single-car garage."

She clapped her hands together. "Then all I'll need is a car working well enough to put in there."

"Car troubles, too?"

She shrugged.

He made another note to take a look at her car.

"You're going to fix that, too?"

"I may know a thing or two about engines. All part of being a handyman."

"Anyone ever tell you, you're an angel?"

He belly-laughed at that. "My mom used to call me a little devil, but, no, definitely not an angel."

"Well, to me, today you are an angel I desperately needed. My friend Lissa would tell me that God is good even when bad things happen. I'm working on believing that."

"I can assure you, it's true." Although he'd had his moments of doubt as well.

He turned in a circle, surveying the yard, the neighbor's yards, stamping the landscape onto his memory. If Flynn had some goon spying on Rita, Daniel needed to know each and every possible hiding place.

"Anything else you'd like done?" He walked with her around the side of the house, taking in the crumbling sidewalk that led from the side door to the shed. The basement didn't have any egress windows so access would be difficult.

"That's more than enough. Thank you and whatever organization sponsored this contest."

"I'll pass that on." They reached the front of the house. "There's one other important item that's part of your winnings."

"More?"

"You get a full security system." Courtesy of the Rochester Police Department. He was thrilled when they threw that in. It would make his job, and anyone else providing security, much easier. And it would make bugging the home easier as well so Wallace and Steinbach across the street would be able to monitor the home.

And Rita's conversations. He hated that part, but if she was in cahoots with the Flynns, it was necessary.

She blinked, and her eyes grew glassy. "A security system?"

"The best there is."

"I don't have money to pay a monthly fee."

"It's covered by the contest for up to a year." If that wasn't okay with his boss, then Daniel would fork it out to ease his conscience about wire-tapping the place. "After that, it's up to you if you want to pay the monthly fee, but regardless, you keep the equipment."

"Then that's the first thing I want done." She stood and brushed off the back of her jeans. "When can you start?"

"I've got it in my pickup so I can begin right now, if you want."

"Please begin. Then maybe tonight, I'll get some sleep."

Guilt might keep him awake. He believed Rita was completely innocent, but the investigation needed to cover every angle, and that meant not only protecting her, but spying on her as well.

Why did she say that? Rita mentally chastised herself. Daniel didn't know, didn't *need* to know her troubles, but he certainly had a way that made her want to spill everything to him. She'd give Lissa a call later in the day, let her know what was going on. It would be good to have someone to talk to. Someone who would pray with and for her.

But before then, she had some research to do. When she'd met Robert, she'd taken him at face value, believed that he was a surgeon. In a town filled with medical personnel, that was an easy lie to believe, so she hadn't questioned it. Lesson learned.

With Momma engrossed in the latest episode of *The Virginian*, Rita woke her computer and did a search on Mayo's website under cardiovascular surgery. Twenty-five doctors were listed, none by the name of Robert Smithson. She was an idiot! How easy it would have been to look him up. He'd banked on her believing him, and he collected with interest.

She was not going to make the same mistake with Daniel Winter. Sure, Detective Cramer had checked him out, but that didn't mean she couldn't. She typed in the website listed on his business card: www.WinterHandyman.com.

Winter Handyman Services, LLC. came up. The top of the page highlighted his license number and phone number. The About page had a photo of Daniel shaking hands with a customer. It talked about him growing up in the trade, that his business was accredited, and that he had fifteen-plus years of experience. Another page highlighted glowing reviews, along with images of the before and after pictures.

But a website did not prove his legitimacy. Anyone could put up a website. The business had a Facebook page, but she couldn't find a personal page for him. LinkedIn showed him connected with people in many walks of life, including a lot of cops, even Detective Cramer. Was that significant?

She checked the Better Business Bureau. The business was there, it was accredited, and had numerous glowing reviews. Then she checked out his license number. Also, legit.

She googled the contest her momma had entered. There was her mom's name highlighted as winner. Huh.

It was real.

The doorbell rang, and her stomach growled as she went to answer it. She looked through the peephole. A courier. At least he was dressed as a courier, and Daniel had told her to expect one. Was this how her life was going to be now, doubting everything she saw, fearing every move she made?

She lifted a prayer before opening the door and stepping outside. The man handed her an envelope which she opened cautiously while on the steps. She pulled out a document and read through it.

Daniel was real. The remodeling win was real.

She sighed, long and loud, releasing pent-up stress.

She could trust Daniel Winter. Today, that was a blessing.

Her stomach growled again, reminding her not only that it was way past time to eat, but that her shelves were nearly empty. She'd planned to go shopping today. *Ha!*

She'd just have to make do with what they had. If she didn't make lunch, Momma would forget to eat. As it was, she was becoming pickier as the months dragged on. All she wanted was sweets, and that was the last thing she needed.

Rita perused the cupboard. Some generic canned soups that didn't appeal to her either. The fridge was almost as empty as Old Mother Hubbard's cupboard, which meant, after making a handful of peanut butter sandwiches for Momma, herself, and Daniel—not that he expected it, but it seemed the right thing to do—she'd have to humble herself and make a trek to the food shelf today after all.

After she'd met Robert, he'd bought groceries, gas, anything she needed so that she didn't have to work. At that time, she'd just begun an online training course for a work-from-home job. Robert had made that course unnecessary with his promises to marry her and house her momma. She'd resume those classes ASAP.

How quickly and easily she'd given in to him, allowing him to strip away her defenses and her common sense with his flattery and generosity and promises, effectively separating her from other people and hindering her from making new relationships.

Like he'd been molding her for his own purposes.

Had he been grooming her to join them?

She shivered at the thought. She might be gullible, but drug trafficking? No way.

So now, she was back to being poor and hungry. But that was certainly better than being in jail.

Nothing was better at erasing pride than being hungry. After lunch, she and Momma would go for a walk, the little wagon she'd found at a garage sale in tow. *If* Momma would go for a walk. Walking was healthy for both of them.

But was it safe?

Were the Flynns watching her every move? What about the police? They said they'd be keeping a close eye on her.

The fact was, she had to go shopping. Having once lived in the Twin Cities metro area, she'd taken self-defense classes, although her skills had never been challenged.

She prayed they wouldn't be necessary today.

What she'd give to wring Robert's neck for stealing her freedom. For him to act so in love while plotting how to use her, he must be pure evil. If only she could turn off the memories, the feelings from the good times they'd shared together. How long would it take to recover from betrayal?

Nope. No more feeling sorry for herself. That would do neither her nor her mother any good. She wasn't one to lie down and give up. Despite this mess "Robert" had dumped her into, she planned to live, and that began with going for a walk with her mom to get groceries.

But first, they needed to have lunch so Momma would have energy for the walk.

She slapped together sandwiches with peanut butter and strawberry jelly. She set up a TV tray for Momma then brought a couple sandwiches and an ice water out to Daniel, who was up on a ladder installing what looked like a camera by her entry.

"Hungry?" She held up the lunch to him.

"For me?"

"I don't see anyone else out here."

He grinned and climbed down. "Thank you. This is exactly what I've been craving."

"I'd give you more, but my cupboards are pretty bare. Momma and I are going to take a walk when she's done eating, get some groceries."

"A walk, huh?" Something subtle changed in his demeanor. A stiffness that disappeared as quickly as it came. "Nice day to walk." He bit into the sandwich. "Delicious."

"It's just peanut butter and jelly."

"That I didn't have to make, which makes it delicious."

She shrugged. "You're welcome, I guess." Shaking her head, she went back into the house. No surprise, Momma had taken one bite out of her sandwich. "Momma, you have to eat more."

She threw the sandwich onto the carpeted floor. "That's what I think of your sandwich."

Rita breathed in sharply through her nose, then blew it out, and repeated the process slower, two additional times. "Momma, what would you like?"

"I want a cookie."

A cookie. Right. That wasn't going to happen, but Rita might be able to fake it.

She picked up the sandwich from off the floor and hurried to the kitchen. She threw that one away then made another sandwich. This time she cut it in a circle, pinched the edges of the bread until they stuck together, then pressed raisins into the bread on both sides. It was worth a try.

She plated the "cookie" and poured a glass of milk and brought both to the living room. "Here's your cookie. It's your favorite."

Momma's eyes lit up as she grabbed the sandwich and took a

big bite. "Yum!" In seconds, she'd devoured the entire sandwich.

If only that would work a second time too, but this disease was never that accommodating. Times like this made her feel like the parent. She was constantly teaching, encouraging her mother much as a parent does a toddler. The difference was the toddler would eventually learn. With Momma, what she learned this second would be forgotten the next. Digression instead of progression. So, each moment had to be cherished.

Even if the moments were shrouded with fear, thanks to the Flynns, she wasn't about to let them control her life anymore.

Chapter Four

Daniel climbed up on the roof of the house, not only to check the shingles, but to survey the landscape. Fortunately, most of the homes in this neighborhood were rambler style and easy to see over.

What would be the optimal places for the Flynn goons to hide for their own surveillance?

He mentally mapped out the area as he checked the roof. No surprise, the shingles needed to be replaced. A second layer had already been added, which meant the roof needed the full job. Tear off and replace. Considering that the roof gave him the best vantage point, this was the perfect task for him.

Movement below caught his attention. Rita headed for her shed. Moments later, she tugged a faded red wagon from the lopsided building. She must be taking that on her walk to the grocery store.

She brought the wagon around to the front of the house, went inside, and came out moments later with her mother. Gladys, dressed in neon yellow pants and shirt, walked with a cane. She'd never get lost in that getup.

"Going somewhere?" He called down from the roof.

Rita's hand flew to her heart as she looked up at him, but Gladys kept walking. "Don't startle me like that."

"Oops, sorry." He should have considered she'd already be on edge. "Just making sure it's okay for me to work here while you're gone."

Her eyebrows pinched together. "Isn't that normal?"

"It is, but I never assume."

"Something I need to learn, apparently." She glanced back at her mom turning onto the city sidewalk. "Better catch up with the walking banana and turn her in the right direction."

Daniel laughed. "Good luck. When you get back, I'll update you on my plans."

While Rita jogged to catch up to her mom, he called the officer taking the day shift in the apartment across the street.

"They're on the move, Wallace. The mother is dressed like a yellow highlighter. You can't miss them."

"Got it," she replied and hung up.

Wallace and Steinbach were posing as a married couple in the apartment. Not only would they be visibly surveilling the house, they'd be listening in and had settled on the code word "Rugby" if he needed help quickly without alerting the Flynns.

The wagon rattling behind her, Rita caught up to her mom and gestured toward the opposite direction. Gladys vehemently shook her head and continued on her way. Again, Rita stopped her and motioned behind them. Gladys crossed her arms and seated herself on the sidewalk like a petulant child.

Oh boy. That had to be what Rita had worried about, what kept her from going to a safe house. How could he help?

He climbed down his ladder and hurried to where Gladys sat firmly on the concrete, tears rolling down her face.

She caught sight of Daniel and wiped a hand across her nose. "She's making me go the wrong way. I don't know that way."

With a big sigh, Rita plopped down in the wagon, her legs

stretched in front of her on the sidewalk, and looked up at the cloud-mottled sky. "The grocery store we usually go to is that way. I can't go there today." She shook her head and sniffled. "I can't leave her home alone, but we need to eat." Her fists clenched, she kicked at a weed-filled hole in the sidewalk and grunted out. "I can't do this anymore."

"Hey." He knelt in front of her, ignoring Gladys's sobs. "I know you don't know me, and have no reason to trust me, but if you'd rather go shopping on your own, I can keep an ear and eye on your mom. I happen to have monitors in my truck, part of the security system I'm adding to your home, so I can work and watch her." That was one way to get the monitors set up with her permission.

Rita's head slowly angled toward him, her expression a mixture of unbelief and relief. "You'd do that for me?"

He shrugged.

And she looked at him sideways, her eyes squinted, as if she didn't trust his motives. Not that he blamed her. "I don't think that's in the handyman job description."

"Maybe not, but it is in the *son* description my parents gave me."

She sniffled and wiped an arm across your nose. "Sounds like you have pretty good parents."

"The best."

Her head swiveled toward her mom—who'd stopped sobbing, but sat sullenly, her bottom lip protruding out, and her arms crossed—then back to Daniel. "Guess I don't have much of a choice." Squaring her shoulders, she stood then knelt in front of Gladys. "Momma, time to go home. Your favorite stories are on."

And just like that, Gladys got off the ground, her eyes bright. "Then let's get going. I don't want to miss anything." She ambled toward the house.

"You won't." Rita said under her breath and looked to Daniel. "Thank you."

Together, they followed Gladys back to the house. Once there, Daniel set up the monitoring system as Rita got her mom settled.

"You're good to go." He showed Rita his tablet that displayed images of each room in the house.

She shivered. "That's a little creepy, isn't it?"

"Some say creepy, others like the safety element, and it'll give you a little bit of freedom."

"I suppose." She nibbled at her lower lip. "You'll stay close."

"Won't leave the property."

She nodded. "It is what it is, and I need to head out before the place closes."

With Gladys firmly ensconced in front of the television, Daniel stepped outside with Rita who locked the door then gave him a spare key.

"I won't be long." She hurried down the sidewalk, then aimed in the opposite direction her mother had wanted to go. He may not know Rita well at all, but knowing the path that lay ahead for her and her mother broke his heart. Nothing was tougher than watching loved ones lose themselves.

He kept an eye on Rita as he climbed back on the roof, then he called Wallace. "Little hiccup. Dunlap's on the move without her mom." He knelt on the edge of the roof, pretending to inspect as he surveilled the area and waited for Wallace to emerge from the apartment. Moments later, she appeared wearing jogging pants and a T-shirt. She remained outside the apartment, stretching, but Daniel knew she was keeping an eye on Rita.

A few feet before Rita reached a corner, Wallace began her jog on the opposite side of the street, maintaining enough of a distance so Rita shouldn't hear her or get suspicious, yet close enough where she'd be able to see if Rita turned off.

Then both were out of his sight.

While keeping an eye on the neighborhood, and his tablet, he removed his tape measure from his tool belt and took measurements of the roof, periodically checking for soft spots that would involve more work. Then he called Compound Lumber to place an order for shingles and other materials needed to redo the roof.

The problem now was, his order wouldn't arrive until tomorrow, so he wouldn't do removal until then. Without a roofing task, he couldn't remain up here and keep his cover, so he messaged Wallace, "Heading down," to let her know she'd lost her extra set of eyes. But now was also the perfect time to add a camera to the storage shed. The sooner that wreck came down, the better.

The door was unlocked—he mentally scrawled "add a lock" on his to-do list—so he let himself in. All that was inside was a lawn mower, snow shovel, and some tools.

He checked his phone for updates on Rita.

Nothing.

Then he realized he'd forgotten to do his most important task of all.

Get on his knees and pray.

Someone was following her. Rita knew it without looking back. She felt in her bones that she was being watched. She upped her speed, tugging the rattily wagon behind her, and finally spotted the food shelf a block away. The rest of the way there, she prayed for protection, while trying not to hurl mental darts at "Robert" for putting her in this mess.

At last, she reached the building and rushed inside, trying not to look harried. Judging by the sweat seeping from her pores, she was certain she'd failed.

Keeping the wagon with her, she walked past a shelving unit where she wouldn't be seen from the window and stood there, willing her breathing to slow to normal. How dare Robert do this to her? Funny how quickly those euphoric feelings of love had turned into fiery feelings of hate.

She stood at the end of an aisle and concentrated on breathing, on calming her heart. There was no way she could walk home on her own. Not today. But who could she call? Robert had been her best friend—only friend—in town. Lissa lived over two hours away in a Twin Cities' suburb with her new husband and stepdaughter. They spoke on the phone often, but rarely saw each other, not with Rita's new responsibilities. She'd been her momma's caregiver since arriving, so she rarely got out. The only place she ever went was to church, and Robert had accompanied them there. Thanks to him, and probably intentionally, she knew no one.

Other than Daniel.

She'd asked so much of him already, but she also wasn't a dummy. If Robert's family was as bad as the police claimed, she could be in real danger. And if something happened to her, what would become of Momma?

She retrieved Daniel's business card from her wallet and stared at it. Would he walk her home, or even better, give her a ride so they weren't out in the open? Would he look at her as a helpless female in need of rescuing? She hated that she felt like a victim, even though that was exactly what she was.

Suck it up, girl. Give him a call.

She dialed his number while formulating an excuse.

"Winter Handyman Services, how can I help you?"

That businesslike answer alone reassured her.

"Hi, uh, Daniel, it's Rita." She tried to speak calmly, but knew she didn't succeed. "I'm in a bit of a bind. I needed more groceries than I can pull in my wagon. Is it possible for you to come give me a ride?"

"Hey, glad to help. But what about your mom?"

Rita groaned. Why hadn't she thought this through? No way would Momma walk with Daniel. "I'm five minutes away from home. She'll be fine at home alone." She hoped.

"If you're sure."

"Positive."

Not really, but what choice did she have?

"Where are you at?"

She winced as she gave the name of the place and the address. Admitting she picked up groceries at the food pantry embarrassed her, especially around people who seemed to accomplish so much with their lives. If she weren't so skilled at finding love in the wrong people, she'd be someone too.

That would change. She'd restart the online class so she could work from home. No one or no circumstances were going to keep her down.

While waiting, she hurried through the food bank, taking only what she and Momma really needed to survive. Survival was more than food. It was surrounding yourself with people who loved you. Somehow, with Robert's influence, this extrovert had cut herself off from everyone. How had she not seen that before? Oh, he was cunning. Someday, she planned to let him know exactly what she thought of him.

The catch in Rita's voice alerted Daniel to hurry. His tablet in hand, he left the shed, his project half finished, and ran to his pickup. Only then did he take a moment to message Wallace.

> – Rita called.
> Sounds scared.
> Anything? –

> – Nothing suspicious.
> Waiting outside the food bank. –

That didn't ease Daniel's concern—the Flynns wouldn't have eluded capture for so long if they were obvious, and he'd learned to trust gut instinct. He contacted Officer Steinbach across the street, let him know what was up, then keyed the address into his phone. As Rita claimed, the food bank wasn't far from here, still he floored the accelerator, disregarding the speed limit.

Less than five minutes later, he pulled into a space in front of the building and hurried inside. He checked all the aisles until he spotted the wagon overflowing with bagged goods. He took a second to calm his breathing before approaching Rita, then he handed her the tablet showing that Gladys hadn't moved from her chair.

Rita sighed out, "Thank you." The woman was clearly terrified.

"Glad to help. You ready to go?"

She just nodded, her arms hugging her upper body as if to

disguise the shakes.

It wasn't working.

He escorted Rita out of the building and opened the front door of his pickup. She climbed in without saying another word while he quickly loaded the food bags into the pickup bed.

Had Wallace spooked Rita, or was it something or someone else?

Silence filled the cab, driving back to Rita's home. His gaze roamed looking for anything amiss, anything that alerted his radar. He'd make no assumptions. Nothing stood out, but that didn't mean anything. More than ever, he knew they had to be vigilant.

And that meant he had to finish installing the security system today.

When they arrived at the house, Rita remained outside, her shakes had calmed considerably. "That was unbelievably nice. Thank you."

He shrugged. "Glad to help, but now it's time to get back to work. I'd like to finish installing your security system today, and that means coming into your house again."

"You have full access, if you don't mind Momma flirting with you."

He grinned. "Doesn't hurt the ego any."

"Seriously?" She wrinkled her nose, which looked awfully cute on her. "But I do have another question for you."

"Okay?"

"Do you happen to know where I can get a dog?"

"A dog?" Hmm, not a bad idea. Would be an added measure of safety, but Daniel Winter, the remodeler, wouldn't know that was what she wanted. "You want a support animal for your mom?"

"I hadn't thought of that but, I'm feeling . . . I don't know." She looked up and down the street and crossed her arms over her chest. "I feel like I'm being watched, and it's giving me the creeps. I think having a big, ferocious-looking dog might deter any bad guys."

"I might know someone." A good friend trained dogs for the force and would likely point Daniel in the right direction.

"Really? Oh, good. That gives me peace. Between your security system and the dog, maybe I'll get sleep soon."

"I'll call him right now."

"Thank you. And I'll check on Momma, see how she's doing." Rita went into the house.

Only when he heard the door latch did he pull out his phone. It rang as he walked to his pickup. He didn't need Rita to hear this conversation.

"Daniel." Keith answered. "What's up man?"

He covered his mouth so lipreaders couldn't discern what he was saying. "I'm back on the force in Rochester."

"Good to hear, man. The city needs guys like you."

"That's my hope." Daniel leaned against his truck, his gaze never still. It caught Wallace jogging back from the store. They made eye contact but otherwise didn't acknowledge each other. "Anyway, I was wondering where I can find one of your rejects. I've got someone wanting a guard-slash-service dog."

"Hmm. Let me think."

"Add this to your equation: the woman has no expendable money."

"Dude, seriously?"

"Dead."

Daniel could hear his friend's fingers drumming.

"Fine. I know just the dog. It's a shepherd mix, has only three legs. Lost it in some nutjob's animal trap. He looks and barks ferocious as all get out, and will protect its owner. Don't let its missing leg fool you. But the owner has to be prepared to be licked to death."

"Sounds like exactly what I'm looking for. When can I pick him up?"

"Whenever you want. The wife will love me for donating a dog to you."

Daniel laughed. "I'll be over tomorrow night. Tell your wife, thank you."

"Believe me, she's saying thank *you*!"

With a chuckle, he hung up then retrieved the rest of the supplies for the security system and wiretapping from his pickup. Time to get to work adding protection to this house. No one would die on his watch.

Again.

"Cricket? Who names their German shepherd Cricket?" Per Daniel's instructions, Rita knelt in front of the dog in order to not look as intimidating. She also avoided eye contact with him, while holding out her fist to let Cricket sniff. The dog's tail began wagging faster than summer fled in Minnesota, so she took that as an okay to pet him on his back. Daniel had told her the all-black dog looked mean as a bear, and he was right. The poor thing probably couldn't wait to escape the humiliation of its name.

"How would you like a new name?" She ruffled its fur.

The three-legged canine licked her in answer.

"Cricket," Daniel said sternly, and the dog backed down, his head lowered. "Good boy." He petted the dog, and the tail began wagging again.

Rita rubbed the dog's ears and finally looked it in the eye. "What do you think of the name Brutus?"

The dog backed away.

Okay, not that. "Then how about Thor?"

It just cocked its head, as if she were crazy. Smart dog.

"Fine, then, how about Samwise?" The dark barked and the tail took off again. "Samwise it is." She continued petting and didn't mind a few licks to the face. The nice thing about dogs was, they loved unconditionally. Unlike people.

"You a *Lord of the Rings* fan?" Daniel knelt beside her as dog and owner became familiar with each other.

"Of course. Isn't everyone?"

"Ha! Not my ex-fiancée."

"Which is probably why she's an *ex*-fiancée, right?"

"Probably." He grinned.

"Samwise was my favorite, especially in the movies."

"Really? Not Aragorn? All the women I know are in love with him."

"All the women you know?" She giggled, which felt really good in this stress-filled time. "Almost sounds like you have a harem."

"I've got a few sisters. Three to be exact, and they all crushed on Aragorn."

"He wasn't bad. At all. But he was groomed to be a hero. Samwise wasn't. He was a friend, a loyal man who stood by Frodo and wasn't afraid to tell him he was messing up. Frodo may have thrown the ring into the fires of Mordor, but he never would have gotten there without Samwise."

"Wise analysis and a perfect name for your new friend."

"Where'd his leg go?"

Rita looked behind her at her momma wearing a nightgown and fuzzy blue slippers. Guess this was as good a time as any to introduce the housemates.

"Momma, meet Samwise."

Momma shuffled toward the dog and Samwise immediately stiffened. His ears grew taut.

"Stop there, Momma."

"I wanna pet the dog." She whined like a six-year-old.

"You can, but Samwise needs to trust you first. Stay there." With her eyes, Rita motioned for Daniel to stay with the dog. She retrieved a chair from the kitchen and had Momma sit down. "Now hold out your fist. Don't look him in the eye, okay?"

"But he has pretty eyes."

"Yes, he does, but he sees that as a challenge. Look down at your slippers instead."

"My slippers?" Momma looked down. "Oh, aren't they a pretty blue? These are my favorite."

While Momma was distracted, Rita stretched her momma's arm out, closing her fingers into a fist. "Come here, Samwise." She patted her leg, and the dog sauntered over, still unsure of the woman and her goofy slippers, but he sniffed her hand, and his tail did a little wag.

"Good boy." Rita petted his back. "Okay, Momma, you can pet Samwise here." She guided Momma's hand to the back and to the sides, and his tail started fanning the room.

"He likes me." Momma continued petting him. He licked her face and she giggled. "Good doggie."

He barked a happy bark.

"But where's his leg?"

Back to that again.

Explaining what really happened might distress her momma,

so she softened the story. "He lost it at his old home."

"Then someone should find it. He wants his leg back." Momma got up quickly. "I'm going to go look for it." She shuffled toward her bedroom.

Rita just shook her head. "Every day is an adventure."

"I see that." Daniel nodded toward the door. "Time for me to head out. I'll be back bright and early tomorrow. You know how to set the alarm?"

"I've got it."

"Okay. Good."

"And with Samwise, I'm doubly covered." The dog remained at her side, already loyal, as she walked Daniel to the front door. "Thank you. Finding me a dog was very kind."

He shrugged. "I just happened to know someone who wanted to find a new home for the guy. It was a win for both of you."

"Please pass along my gratitude."

"I'll do that. Goodnight."

He left and Rita locked the door after him, then set the alarm.

Only then did she realize how exhausted she was. Had it only been two days ago that she thought she was about to be proposed to? *Ha!* What a fool she'd been. And then Daniel shows up, promising the security she needed.

She didn't believe in coincidence—that was the old Rita—but she did believe that God could and would do everyday miracles, and she was claiming this one. The chapter with Robert was over and done with, and though her heart ached like crazy for its loss, she would not dwell on it. Couldn't dwell on it.

With all the security measures now in place, she planned to go to bed and sleep until Momma woke her, which could be ten minutes or ten hours from now.

She donned her flannel pajamas, climbed into bed, and read

a few chapters from the Bible before turning out the light. She offered thanks for revealing the truth about Robert to her and for the protection offered by the police and by Daniel. *Yes, God is good.*

Images of a wedding flashed in front of her eyes. She was the bride, Robert the groom, and every guest held a vase. And then the police burst into the church arresting everyone, including her, leaving her momma alone, crying hysterically.

A song rang from the speakers, quieting Momma.

Rita's eyes flickered open, and the song continued.

Her phone.

Robert's ringtone.

Wasn't he in jail? Should she answer?

No. That would be stupid, in spite of her intense desire to tell him off. If he left a message, she'd give it to the cops.

Her heart racing to the beat of the ringtone, she waited until it quieted, then seconds later her phone dinged indicating she had a voicemail. She signed into voicemail and listened.

A man spoke with a Southern drawl that was similar to Robert's voice—the one that had enchanted her— yet deeper.

His father.

A chill zipped down her spine, freezing her veins.

"Hello Rita, my dear. It was lovely meeting you a few weeks back, and I'm deeply sorry for what my son has put you through. I have assured Robert that I will keep an eye on you for him until he is released, which I'm anticipating will be soon. Please know that you will not be forgotten."

She wrapped her arms around herself, trying to stop the shivers. Maybe going to a safe house would be the best idea after all.

Chapter Five

"Papa Flynn called her?" Daniel slipped on a black sweatshirt and jeans. "Threatened her?"

Howard grunted. "Oh, he was very careful with his words, but yes, the underlying message was 'Watch your back.' With this escalation, I want to move her."

Daniel sighed. "You can't. It won't work. She's the sole caregiver for her mother—"

"I get that, but this is their lives we're talking about."

"I know, but I understand her point. I witnessed one of those meltdowns yesterday." He pulled his 9mm revolver from his side table drawer. "What I want to know is, why does Papa Flynn care about her? I firmly believe she knew nothing of their plans. All she can do is testify that her boyfriend gave her money to buy a vase. That won't exactly put the guy away."

"You're forgetting one very important detail. She met the father. Logical or not, those who meet Papa Flynn are either recruited or meet mysterious deaths. Leaving her and her mom in that home makes them sitting ducks."

"Not as long as they're on my watch." Daniel secured his 9mm between his jeans and the small of his back, and strapped his .380 around his ankle. Both guns were small enough to easily hide.

"Leave the night surveillance to Wallace and Steinbach. You're no good for her or anyone if you're overtired."

Daniel slumped down on his bed. Howard was right, of course. "I hear you, but know that during the day, I'm not letting her out of my sight."

"Good. You do the protecting, and we'll catch Flynn and his cohorts. It's a team effort."

"Yes, sir."

The question now was, how could he be vigilant about keeping an eye on her without her getting the wrong idea? Guess it didn't matter as long as she remained safe.

With Samwise huffing at her side, Rita checked out the front window to see who had knocked. Daniel. Relief washed through her at the sight of him. Having him around was an added measure of safety.

She opened the door, and he smiled big. "Good morning."

Way too upbeat this early in the morning. No way could she be cheerful after spending another night of sleeplessness, even though she had Samwise lying at her side. She'd never imagined she'd allow a dog in her bed. Last night she'd insisted, and Samwise had gladly complied.

Still, all she could think of was Papa Flynn and his threatening words.

"Are you okay?"

She shook herself back to the present and invited him into the house. "Another sleepless night."

"I'm sorry." He petted an insistent Samwise. "Was it the dog?"

"Samwise is the only reason I got any sleep at all." She

gestured toward her kitchen table. "I know you're here to work, but I could really use some sane adult company for a moment. Can I make you coffee? Breakfast?"

"I'll never turn down either. And I'll take my coffee black."

"What, no fun flavors?" She poured him a fresh-brewed cup then began cracking eggs. "I'm not much of a cook, but I do make a mean scrambled egg."

"Sounds delicious to me." He sipped his coffee and sighed. "Perfection."

Admittedly, she missed going to a local coffee shop for specialty coffee drinks, but that was not in the budget.

"What's on your agenda today?" She poured in a touch of milk and whisked the eggs. Samwise remained vigilant at her side.

"Well, the weather looks good for the next week. I removed the old shingles yesterday, and I'll begin re-shingling today."

Samwise nudged her, begging for attention, so she patted his head. "Would it be possible to add one more item to your list?"

"Sure." He whipped out his notebook. "What would you like done?"

"A fence?" Her nose wrinkled as she asked. Even though she had a little yard, erecting a fence wouldn't be a small thing. But with Samwise, she needed one now.

"Shouldn't be a problem." He scribbled in his notebook then stuffed it in his back pocket. "I want to jump on the roof while the weather's dry, but I can get to the fence once the roof is finished. What kind do you want? Privacy? Chain link?"

"Wouldn't chain link be cheaper?"

"Sure, but a privacy fence is nice to have."

"You wouldn't mind?"

"That's what I'm here for."

"You're a lifesaver." She practically cried. She'd feel even safer with a privacy fence around her backyard.

A look crossed his face that she couldn't interpret, before he grinned. "I rather like that. In the handyman biz, you're not likened to a superhero very often. I'll have to let my sisters know."

"You should." She filled a plate with eggs and handed it to him.

Samwise's ears fell, as if he'd been expecting her to feed him. "Sorry, buddy." She rubbed his ears. "No people food for you." Which meant she needed to make another trip to the store to spend money she didn't have.

"That reminds me." He snapped his fingers. "My buddy gave me food and supplies for Samwise. I'll go get them."

"Eat first. He can wait for his breakfast."

"Don't mind if I do." He bent his head toward the plate.

Was he praying?

Moments later, he looked up, breathed in, and smiled. "Smells delicious."

"It's just eggs."

"That I didn't cook myself." He forked a bite and nodded. "Yep. Delicious."

"It's the least I could do to thank you for your help."

"It's my job." He shrugged. "Where's your mom?"

"Sleeping still." She looked down the hall then back at Daniel. "And I let her sleep. When she's awake, it seems I have to always keep an eye on her. She usually sits in her chair watching shows, but then she'll see something shiny and have to go after it. I turn my back for a second, and she can be gone."

"It's a tough life. You must have had a good relationship, with all you're doing for her."

If he only knew. "The only reason Momma lets me live here

now is because she doesn't remember who I am. Before I got the call from the county about her declining health, I hadn't seen her since I was eighteen when she kicked me out of the house. Truth was, I deserved it."

"But . . . " Daniel stopped himself before he sounded too nosy. "Sorry. None of my business."

Without responding, she sat and sipped at her coffee, nibbled at her eggs. "I know you're wondering how she can't know me when I call her Momma."

He shrugged, and said nothing, hoping it would get her to open up. The more he knew about this woman, the better he could protect her.

"Growing up, she was always Mom or Mother. I can't bring myself to call her Gladys, so I called her Momma, and in her world, that's entirely different. Honestly, though, at this stage I don't think she'd comprehend me saying Mom or Mother either."

"I'm sorry you're going through this, regardless of whether you had a close relationship with her or not. It's a tough thing, and what you're doing now honors her."

"You really think so?" She peered at him over the top of her coffee cup.

"I know so."

"Thanks. After the couple of days I've had, I needed to hear that."

He ate the last of his eggs. "And I need to get to work. The roof could be a weeklong project." Actually, it shouldn't take that long, as the roof wasn't large, but he needed to stretch out his time here as much as he could, at least until they had Papa Flynn apprehended.

He got up to put his plate in the sink, but Rita took it from him. "With all you're doing for me, the least I can do is take care of your dishes."

"I won't argue. Dish soap and I don't get along."

"I'll bet your mom loved you." A smile broke through on her weary face.

"She didn't care when I said I was allergic. Go figure." He grinned as he hurried out the door to his pickup. He gathered the dog care items he'd purchased last night and brought them to the house. He knocked and waited a few seconds before the door flung open.

"You really didn't have to knock." She took the bag of dogfood from him and waved him inside.

"My mother would be upset if I didn't."

"Sounds like your mom is something special."

"She is. I'm fortunate." He set the crate filled with other supplies on the floor just inside the door. "Now, back to work." He headed outside.

"Hey, Super-Handyman."

Oh, she did not just go there. Wincing, he turned back. "Yeah?"

"Thank you. You really are a lifesaver."

All he could do was shrug. If only she knew the truth.

Chapter Six

Paint roller in one hand, paint can in the other, Daniel stepped down the sidewalk and looked back at the little rambler he'd been working on these past five-plus weeks. The home had gone from sad to sunny in that short bit of time, while the fall air had gone from humid to chilly. In that time, he'd cut tree branches, replaced the roof, built a privacy fence and a ramp, put an egress window in the basement, built a garden bench. He'd also spent a number of days working on the yard, weeding, laying black dirt, reseeding.

His biggest challenge had been getting her little sedan running. He'd had to take it into the shop for a couple of days, costing him a few hundred dollars out of his own pocket. What she really needed was a new-to-her vehicle. That he couldn't provide.

Painting had taken an entire week because he took his time power washing, repairing, caulking, priming, and taping off windows. On the little rambler, it should have taken half as long, but with Papa Flynn on the loose, he needed to stretch out his time here.

Rita claimed she felt like she was being watched all the time, which was no surprise given the fact that she was under constant surveillance by the Rochester Police Department. Otherwise, there'd been no sign of Papa Flynn. No more phone calls. Nothing suspicious. No doubt, Flynn was attempting to lull all of them to sleep so he'd catch them unguarded.

Flynn didn't know that Daniel was a pit bull when it came to protecting others.

Maybe the key was to make it look like they were relaxing. Daniel would bring that up at the next team meeting.

In the meantime, though, Daniel had one more major project to work on, and this one would likely take him into November. Hopefully by Thanksgiving, Papa Flynn would be behind bars, and they all would have something to be thankful for.

The front door of the house opened, and Rita stood in its entry. "Are you just going to stand there gawking, or are you going to come in and have some cookies?"

"Cookies?"

"Homemade."

"You're talking my language." He set down the paint can and laid the brush on top. "But first, come on out. Look at your place."

"You're done?"

"Put the last stroke of paint on five minutes ago."

Samwise snuck past Rita and bolted toward him. He jumped up, but Daniel turned away without speaking, hopefully discouraging the action.

"Sorry about that." Rita grimaced and locked the door behind her. She hurried to his side and looked back. "Oh, my!" She fluttered her fingers in front of her eyes.

Tears? For a paint job?

"It's beautiful. I can't wait to show Momma."

"She still sleeping?"

"Later and later every morning. I relish the time she's asleep, but then I feel guilty for not waking her."

"One thing we learned from taking care of Grandma is that you can't hold on to guilt. We were all doing our best in caring for her, and you're doing your best. She's well taken care of."

"Do you think Momma realizes that? Do you think she'll finally love me, even if she doesn't realize it's me caring for her?"

He resisted putting an arm around her, his heart breaking at her question. Love couldn't be bought, no matter how much someone paid for that love. Real love was given away without condition.

What had happened in Rita's childhood that taught her love needed to be purchased?

Why did that even concern him?

Samwise butted between the two of them, taking care of any urge Daniel had to hold her.

She cleared her throat, probably feeling as uncomfortable as he did. "What's next?"

Thankful for the change of subject, he gestured toward the weed-filled border gardens. "Would you like fall flowers? Most stores have deals on mums right now."

"Oh, what a good idea, but that's something I can do—I need to do myself. It's time I take ownership in this house as well. Seeing it spruced up like this makes me want to make it pretty. Before, I felt that adding flowers was like bringing a porcupine to a hairdresser. Futile."

"Would your momma like to go shopping, too? We could make an afternoon of it?" She'd even become used to his pickup and often asked to go for rides, all under the guise of going on a date. But he'd do whatever it took.

Rita laughed, something that was happening with more frequency, and he loved hearing it.

"You do realize that if we go out together in your pickup, it will be an official date for Momma and, chances are, she'll wear her highlighter-yellow outfit for the occasion."

"Then we won't have to worry about losing her."

"That's for sure." She looked back at the house, and her smile faded. "I suppose you're almost done here, aren't you?"

"Well, I do have to build the garage yet."

"That should take a while, shouldn't it?"

"A week or so." In reality, probably two days. The concrete had been poured and cured already, before the temperatures turned colder. Putting up the structure would be like building with toy blocks. Not a difficult task for him. But he'd take his time, as he'd done with all the other projects.

There had to be work inside he could do, too.

The dog nudged his hand, and Daniel petted the animal's course fur. "What about a doghouse? Maybe a miniature version of your momma's place." That could occupy him for a whole day, if he let it.

She clapped her hands together. "I love that idea!" She knelt and rubbed Samwise's face between her hands. "What do you think of that, boy? Your very own house!"

He barked his approval.

"And maybe I could give Daniel a hand." She looked up at him, her brows raised.

How could he say no? "Sure."

"Thank you." Donning a big smile, she got up. "I figure if I'm going to be caring for Momma and her home, I should learn how to take care of the home too, right?"

"Good idea." He shrugged, not liking how much he enjoyed her smile. He'd been afraid of this, spending too much time around women always turned his emotions upside down. He'd hoped after the last debacle it wouldn't happen again.

He just had to be diligent about focusing on his job. But how would he manage that if Rita was working right alongside him?

Diligence and a whole bunch of prayer. That had been the missing ingredient last time he'd become attracted to someone. He'd tried handling it with his own strength rather than giving it up to God. He'd thought he could be their hero, when he wound up being the goat. This time, he wouldn't make the same mistake.

"Momma, come outside with us." Rita handed her mother a jacket. "I'm helping Daniel build a doghouse for Samwise." Who, as usual, had parked himself at Momma's feet.

No surprise, Momma didn't move. She just stared at the television. More and more, all she wanted to do was sit. Even getting her to go to the bathroom was becoming a chore.

Well, there was one other way to get her momma moving. "Samwise. Outside?"

The dog jumped up and pawed at Momma, diverting her attention from the TV. He yipped at her and turned toward the side door leading into the backyard. Momma remained sitting, so Samwise barked this time.

"Okay, okay, I'm coming, I'm coming." With some effort, Momma got up from her rocker and shuffled behind Samwise to the door. Those two had become inseparable, and Samwise had become the babysitter Rita needed.

With the dog at her side, Momma shuffle-walked to the garden bench Daniel had built and sat. Only then did Samwise make full use of being outside and run around the yard, enjoying the freedom and the cooler weather.

When Rita had asked Daniel to build a fence, she'd assumed it would be for the dog, but now she realized how wonderful it was for her momma as well. When outside, Rita no longer had to watch Momma every single second. Suddenly, Rita had new freedom.

Which also gave her some breathing space.

The very space Robert had promised her.

Had it only been five weeks since she had learned the truth about him? Somedays it felt like it was only yesterday she'd been hearing future wedding bells, and she'd have her moments of tears, missing him. Hating him. Then other days, like today, Robert seemed a million years ago and, with Daniel around, her hope had been restored.

Problem was, she'd felt the same way when she'd met Robert. He'd given her hope then yanked it out from beneath her feet. She certainly wouldn't be gullible enough to listen to those feelings again.

"In your happy place?" Daniel's voice broke through Rita's musing.

She smiled. That had been happening a lot more lately, too. Easily and freely. "Just thinking about what a blessing you've been. If Momma hadn't been so fixated on entering contests, you wouldn't be here, and I'd be wallowing in my own pity-party over Robert's deception."

"Yeah." He shrugged and turned to the workbench he'd set up outside. "Glad I could be here to help." He pushed a piece of wood through some kind of electric saw. How he didn't cut off his fingers, she didn't know.

"How can I help? Other than that machine that separates fingers from your hands."

Daniel laughed at that. "Haven't lost a finger yet. It's got safeguards, but you also have to pay attention to what you're doing. Come on. Give it a try. I'll guide you through it."

"You promise I won't lose any fingers?"

"As long as you pay attention, I promise."

She propped her hands on her hips. "Sure, blame me."

"Get on over here." He grinned and waved her over.

Reluctantly, she went to his side, and gulped. "Okay. What do I do?"

"Safety first." He handed her a pair of oversized, clear glasses.

"For when I want to attract a man's attention." She put them on and batted her eyelashes.

"Works every time." He laughed. "But seriously, seeing a woman covered in sawdust, working with power tools, is pretty sexy."

"Well, in that case, I'm here to learn."

"I knew you would be." He pointed to a pencil line drawn on the piece of wood he had secured on a metal horse. "I've already got it measured, the blade set to the right depth and angle, so all you have to do is follow the straight line to make a cut." He picked up the wicked looking circular saw by the red handle. "This has the safety switch and the trigger." He pointed them out. "And this front handle helps stabilize your cutting. All you have to do is rest the base plate flat on the wood. You'll see the line through the hole there, and you align it with the notch."

She inhaled a deep breath and accepted the tool. She rested it on the wood and aligned it. "Okay?"

"Perfect."

She pointed to the metal part covering the blade. "How can it cut if this guard is on?"

"Once it reaches the wood, it slides back. A safety feature so we don't lose our fingers."

"Oh. Gotcha."

He gestured to a black thingy on the handle. "To make it go, you squeeze the trigger. You want to get the blade up to speed before it touches the wood. Then you gently push the blade through, almost letting it pull you. Once it's free of the wood, release the trigger and wait until the blade stops before setting it down. Think you can do it?"

"I . . . " She looked back toward Momma. The dog sat at her feet, so he wouldn't be a distraction. "Let's do it."

"Atta girl. I'll be right here."

She inhaled a deep breath and squeezed the trigger. The blade started spinning and she guided the tool into the wood. As Daniel had said, she didn't really have to push as the tool pulled her forward. All she had to do was follow the line. At last the blade cleared the wood, and the cut piece fell to the ground. She gasped, but held the saw until the blade stopped spinning. Then at last she breathed.

"How'd I do? And should that have fallen?"

He picked up the wood and checked the line. "Perfect. And, yes, it's actually best for the cut piece to fall away."

"So, I did everything right?"

"You still have all your fingers?"

She looked at her hands that once upon a time had always been perfectly manicured. Most importantly, though, every finger was intact. "No blood."

He splayed his hands. "You did it. Easy as making pie."

"I hate making pie."

"You and me both." He carried the wood to a pile of other pre-cut pieces. "How'd you like to use the nail gun?"

She grinned. "I'm ready to learn."

A few hours later, the doghouse was built, and they were all sitting outside beneath the starlit sky by the firepit—another Daniel addition to the yard—roasting hot dogs, making s'mores, and sipping hot cocoa. Momma was content as long as Samwise was at her side. Now this was freedom. This was living.

It almost made her forget about the Flynn family.

A chill zagged down her spine, and she looked around.

She wasn't the only one. Daniel suddenly appeared to be on alert as well. He sat rigid and his gaze seemed to take in their entire surroundings.

Samwise emitted a low growl.

"Let's head on in," Daniel said in a quiet but urgent tone, and practically pushed everyone toward the side door.

"I don't want to go in." Momma whined so the entire neighborhood must have heard.

"Shhh, Momma." Rita tugged on her hand, but Momma yanked it away. "Samwise, help."

The dog appeared to understand as he nudged Momma's hand, and she readily followed him to the house.

Daniel was the last one in, and he backed in through the door. "Set the alarm," he said while locking the door. "And help me make sure the windows are closed and locked."

"What's going on? What did you see?"

"Go," he said sharply and hurried to the bedrooms while she set the alarm.

All she could think of was that Papa Flynn was finally making his move.

Chapter Seven

Shivering, Rita stood back as Daniel took control, as if he'd done this before.

He gathered the family in the living room and shut off the lights, then to Rita he said, "Keep everyone here. I need to make a phone call."

To who? What was going on? And what happened to the Daniel she knew? The easygoing, easy smiling man who didn't let things ruffle him?

His change in demeanor added to her chills. Had she done it again, become attracted to a man—and, yes, she was definitely attracted—who wasn't who he claimed to be?

Something clicked in back of her and voices filled the room, practically propelling her heart out of her chest.

The television.

"Momma, turn that off," she whispered sharply and reached for the remote.

Momma held it away. "I want to watch my stories."

"Fine." Rather than fight for the remote, Rita went behind the TV and pulled the plug.

"I want my stories!" Momma wailed like a toddler.

"She okay?" Daniel reappeared in the room, clutching his phone at his side.

Rita nodded, then realized he probably couldn't see her well in the dark. "She's fine. Just wants the TV on."

"Called Detective Cramer," he said in a clipped tone. "They're on the way."

"Why? Did you see something? Hear something?"

"Not what I saw or heard." He paced the room, going from one window to the next.

"You felt it too."

"I did."

She sat on the couch and cuddled up in a blanket, hoping to get rid of the chill bumps.

An eternity of minutes passed before she saw the red and blue flashing lights outside the house. Before she had time to say anything, Daniel commanded her to lock the door behind him before he bolted outside.

What just happened here?

Part of her wanted to join Daniel outside. She might have if she didn't have to worry about Momma, but she'd finally settled down, and Rita didn't want to stress her out again.

Oh, who was she kidding? No way did she want to go outside. She'd leave that to the professionals.

And Daniel.

But she wasn't worried about him. No doubt, he could take care of himself.

Another eternity of minutes passed before Daniel came inside, along with Detective Cramer.

The officer nodded toward Momma in the rocker. Her eyes were closed, and she seemed relaxed with Samwise at her feet. "Can we speak to you alone?"

"Sure." She led the men down the hallway to her bedroom. As this was the one room she had control over, she'd painted an accent wall fire-engine red, just like the stripes in her hair. She needed some place to express her personality.

They shut the door behind them and both men stood in front of her, the same feet-apart stance, arms hanging loosely at their sides. Eyes dark and focused. She crossed her arms, hoping to regain control. It was as if she'd landed in an episode of *The Twilight Zone*.

"We found this stapled to your light pole." Detective Cramer held a menu, encased in a plastic bag, for *Le Pain* in Rochester. "Does this mean anything to you?"

She swallowed, staring at the menu, hating the warm fuzzies she felt in remembering that evening. "That's the first place Robert, er, William took me on a date."

Detective Cramer's jaw grew tight.

As did Daniel's.

And that gave her more chills. "What does it mean?"

"They're toying with you, Ms. Dunlap. It's meant to convey a few messages. One: they know where you live. Two: they're familiar with your date schedule with William."

"They've been spying on me this entire time?"

"Probably." He cupped his beefy hands on his hips, opening his jacket, showing off his gun. "Question for you, Ms. Dunlap. On your dates with William, did you always go places you really liked? Places that may have been on your bucket list. When you went out, did it seem that he already knew you?"

She gulped. "Yeah. Why?"

The officer sighed. "Because chances are, they were not only watching you, they likely dug into your past to learn what you liked, and to see where your weak spots were."

"Weak spots?" She grabbed a pillow and hugged it. "What do you mean by that?"

"Things you've done that could potentially be blackmail material. Things that could coerce you into joining their team. The Flynns excel at blackmail, Ms. Dunlap. That's how they keep their business going."

"I've been far from perfect," she murmured and peered up at Daniel. Yes, he was just her handyman, but did she want to air her dirty laundry in front of him?

"I'll leave." Daniel seemed to read her thoughts.

"I want you to stay. The more it's out there, the less power the Flynns will have over me, right?"

"It will impact it, yes." Detective Cramer took out a notebook.

She scooted back until the headboard stopped her, and she crossed her legs in front of her. She focused on those crossed legs, hating to see the disappointment in Daniel's eyes. Why that mattered to her, she didn't know. "At my previous job, I . . . I stole files in order to make one employee look bad while making my boyfriend appear to be the right person for a promotion."

"Hmmm." Detective Cramer just grunted.

What did that mean?

Unfortunately, there was more to her story. "The person I hurt was . . . still is, for some reason . . . my best friend. I later learned the guy was sleeping with me just to get the promotion." Oh, she'd been such an idiot, and she'd called Lissa—her friend—naïve. Getting dumped by your so-called boyfriend when you did everything for them, yet being loved on by your best friend whom you'd hurt badly, had been the catalyst for her wanting to learn about Lissa's faith.

Which had then compelled Rita to go home, to her mother. The county welfare people had called her, said Momma had been found wandering the streets of Rochester unable to find her home of thirty-plus years. Only when Rita had arrived home a year ago did she realize the extent of the dementia that had overtaken Momma, so much so, she didn't even recognize her daughter. In the past year, the disease had progressed far too quickly.

"Have you informed anyone else of this action?" Detective Cramer wrote as he spoke.

"Are you kidding? That's a sure way to lose friends and not get jobs."

"Then it's also fodder for blackmail." This from Daniel.

Oh, he must think she was the world's biggest loser. He'd probably pack up his tools and leave, and she wouldn't blame him.

"I'm sorry you're going through this."

Say what? Her head jerked toward Daniel. Instead of malice, she saw compassion in his eyes.

"We've all messed up, Rita. Thanks for sharing that with me."

"You're not angry?"

"You're not the only one blinded by an ex." He looked away.

Interesting. Maybe without the cop here, she'd get Daniel to share his story.

"Now that confession time is over." Detective Cramer slapped his book closed. "I'd like you to pack up some things for you and your mother. "It's clear that the Flynns intended to bring you into their organization. Your past willingness to cheat for a boyfriend at the expense of a friendship and your job made you an excellent candidate."

Rub it in, why don't you? She clutched the pillow tighter, unable to speak, trying to process what Detective Cramer was saying.

"It's a threat, Ms. Dunlap. Your *life* is at risk here, and I insist that we move you to a safe house."

"But what about Momma?"

"She comes with you."

That couldn't happen. Gathering the nerve to speak up for herself, she released the pillow and sat up straight. "You don't understand. Moving her to an unfamiliar location will disorient her, confuse her more than she already is. It'll shorten her life."

"Staying here may also shorten it," Detective Cramer said far too calmly.

She looked to Daniel, who'd remained quiet during this exchange. "I hate dragging you into this more, but you know what I'm talking about. Moving Momma from her home would kill her."

He finally relaxed his stance. "What if I stayed in the house with you?"

"What? No!" She'd worked hard at overcoming the reputation she'd fully earned when living in the Twin Cities area, and would not allow it to be hurt again.

He stood and hovered over her, his arms crossed as if he were a father scolding her. "You shouldn't be here alone."

She got off the bed, tired of feeling like a victim—even if she was.

"Daniel's right," said Detective Cramer, the traitor.

She shot him a look that made him flinch. Good. "I will not live with a man." Again. "Even if it's just for show."

"Ms. Dunlap's right this time." Detective Cramer just got himself back on her good side.

Daniel opened his mouth, as if to object, then clamped it shut. But something else was stewing inside his brain, she could tell by the twitch of his lips.

"We do not have citizens doing the police department's work." Detective Cramer nodded at Daniel. "But if I can't get you to leave your home, I would like to move someone in with you. Perhaps an officer posing as a caregiver for your mother."

"You could do that?" For the first time since they'd hurried inside, she felt a measure of safety.

"Our number one priority is keeping you safe. The second is to end this Flynn trafficking scheme. With your cooperation, we intend to do both."

"I'll do whatever I can to help." Other than moving out of this home.

"We're pleased to hear that." He finally tucked his notebook inside a jacket pocket. "Please be assured, Ms. Dunlap, that I also have officers constantly surveilling your home."

That didn't really assure her—it felt creepy. No wonder she constantly sensed she was being watched.

"Did they see who stapled the menu?"

"We're looking into it."

Nice cop-speak for "We're not going to tell you."

Wait. What about the security system Daniel had installed? She turned to him. "Would your security cameras have captured who did this?"

"We're looking into it," Detective Cramer responded again.

At least they could come up with an original answer. She mimicked the stance of both the officer and Daniel, hoping to convey that she wasn't helpless. Nor was she stupid enough to do her own police work, but she certainly didn't plan to stand back and watch them plod through the case. She wanted it solved now so she and Momma could live in peace. "I want you guys to do more than look into it. I want you to find the dirt bag who did this, so Momma and I can live peacefully again."

"That's the plan, ma'am."

"And don't call me ma'am."

Daniel walked with Howard out to his cruiser, keeping his voice low in case Rita was listening. "Think you'll see anything on that security tape?"

"Sure. Probably some punk kid who was paid a few bucks to prank someone. Probably went through a middleman before it reached the punk. The Flynn gang excels at keeping themselves hidden."

"But the Rochester PD is better. Flynn'll mess up soon, and we'll catch him." Daniel prayed that mess-up would occur before anyone else got hurt. Namely, Rita Dunlap.

He felt for his 9mm revolver in the small of his back. It was there, of course. He'd feel naked without it. They stopped by the cruiser, neither of them letting their gazes rest. "With this threat, can I tell her the truth now? She's certainly not a suspect anymore. The wiretapping should prove that out."

"No, she's not." Howard gripped the roof of the vehicle. "But maintain status quo for now. You never know what she might spill that she's not even aware of."

"I don't like it." Daniel hated this part of the job, hated being dishonest with Rita, hated misleading her—how was he any better than her bogus doctor boyfriend or that scum she worked with in the Twin Cities?

"One more thing." Howard lowered his voice. "There's rumblings from the jail. William's always been the loose end in this operation, and we're trying to pull that string. Apparently, he's not too happy about Rita being targeted. We're working on him to see if he'll rat on his dad."

"And the sister?"

"Still watching her. As far as we can tell, her hands are clean.

Even William insists she's not involved."

"What about my role? Is that going to change with you bringing in someone as caregiver? I promised Rita additional work would be done."

"Maintain for now. With this threat, I plan to add more officers to the team. We'll move Wallace in as caregiver, as she has experience in that role—apparently a brother has early-onset Alzheimer's."

"That's rough."

"Tell me about it."

"She's also familiar with the Dunlaps and their routine. I'll pair someone else with Steinbach."

"Hope this plan works." Daniel looked back at the house that no longer looked sad. At least he'd been able to do that much for Rita and her mother.

"It will." Howard opened his door. "We'll be in touch, and keep me informed."

"Yes sir." He backed away as Howard took off. Now to gauge Rita's mood. Sure, Wallace would be over here tomorrow to act as caregiver, but until then Daniel would not leave Rita alone. If she didn't want him in the house, fine. He'd done surveillance from a vehicle many times before. He'd have no trouble doing it tonight or subsequent nights, if that was what it took.

Rita dropped the drape edge as Daniel strode back toward the house. Those two seemed awfully chummy with each other. She had a bunch of questions for Daniel Winter—if that was really his name—and she had no plans to go to bed until they were all answered.

Like the polite guy he purported to be, Daniel knocked on the front door and didn't just let himself in. She did appreciate that. Before Rob—grrr, when was she going to stop using that name! Before she'd dated *William*, the men she'd chosen had been good-looking but narcissistic. William had been good-looking, and a gentleman.

And a liar.

Was that Daniel's description as well?

She welcomed him into the living room. His gaze wandered through the entire room, it seemed, before landing on Momma's empty rocker.

"I convinced her to go to bed. She didn't need anything else to rile her up. Samwise went with her, of course."

"He's adopted her, hasn't he?"

"And her, him. Never knew she liked dogs. Maybe she didn't know she liked dogs."

"Perhaps." He dug his hands deep into his jeans pockets. "Um—"

"Would you mind staying a while?" She gestured to the two-person table pressed to the wall in the kitchen. "Maybe play a game of cards or something to take the edge off? I'm still spooked."

He smiled. Out of relief, it appeared. "Gladly. I know what Detective Cramer said about me not staying here, but after that threat, I'm not confident in leaving you alone. Even if for a night. I'll sleep out in my truck, if that's what you want."

"Let's play a game and see how the evening works out." She led the way to the table. "About all I know for cards is War. You know that?"

He blew on his fist then rubbed it against his chest. "I happen to be a War expert."

"Ha! Bring it!" She began dealing the entire deck, face down, while tossing out her proposition. "I realized tonight how little I know about you. How about, whoever loses a skirmish—"

"A skirmish?"

"Each of us lays a card, and the higher card wins. That's winning a skirmish."

"Huh. Never knew that before. That counts as my fun fact of the day."

"Not really a fact." Rita grinned while dealing out the final two cards. "Just something I made up right now."

"I think you should coin it."

"Maybe I should trademark it and make a ton of money to support Momma."

"Sounds like a plan." He fiddled with his cards until they were perfectly straight. "Now back to the rules. What happens when I win a skirmish?"

"Well, when you or I win, the loser has to answer a question."

"Fair enough."

"And whoever loses a war has to answer two questions."

"Almost sounds like Truth or Dare."

Her eyebrows shot up. "Seriously?"

"Hey." He raised both hands. "An innocent version, okay?"

"Fine. But no, *not* like Truth or Dare."

"I take it you've played the non-innocent version?"

"Uh-uh. No asking questions until you win the skirmish."

He shrugged. "Had to give it a try."

"Ready?" She gripped the top card on her pile.

He did the same, and they both flipped their cards. Daniel had a four.

She had a five.

"I win!" She took both cards and placed them at the bottom of her pile. "I get to ask the first question." She rubbed her hands together as if preparing to ask something juicy. Those would come later. "Have you ever had a dog?"

He rolled his eyes. "My mom rescued an older Pomsky. Dad and I wanted to hate the thing. Can you think of a more unmanly dog? But he grew on us."

"What's its name?"

"Uh-uh. One question at a time."

"Rats. Thought I'd trip you up."

"I'm far brighter than that."

They both flipped their next cards, and Rita won again.

"There. Now I can legitimately ask what your dog's name was."

"That's not a question. You forfeit your turn."

She opened her mouth to object but decided to give him that one. Maybe the more giving she was now, the more pliable he'd be once they got to the tough questions.

"Fine." She slapped over her next card. A queen. He winced, and she held her breath until he turned his card. A jack.

"That's three in a row." She grinned.

"You rigged the deck before I came in the house."

She waggled her brows. "You'll never know, will you?"

"Caught'cha!" He pointed a finger at her. "You just blew another question."

"I . . . " She thought back, and pounded her fist on the table. "Seriously? You should be an interrogator."

"Not a bad idea." He rubbed a hand over his chin as if deep in thought.

"You won't give me one for the sake of being nice?"

He snorted. "I'm the youngest of four kids. I have three sisters who constantly tried to get me to do favors. I learned how not to give in to them."

"Hmm. Well, you did just answer other questions of mine, so now I'm well ahead, and you still know nothing about me."

He licked his finger and drew a number one in the air. "You win, but that's the last of the freebies."

"We'll see about that."

They both flipped cards, and finally Daniel's beat Rita's.

He rubbed his hands together. "Now to come up with something juicy."

"Hey, I was kind to you."

"Your first mistake." He folded his hands on the table and leaned toward her.

She couldn't help but press back in her chair. He really should have been an interrogator. Her mild-mannered handyman suddenly looked menacing.

"Is that your real hair color?"

She burst into laughter. "The black is. The red, not so much."

"Obviously."

"I've also had purple hair, orange, green—"

"Green?"

"It wasn't pretty, believe me."

"Oh, I believe you."

"But I actually liked the purple."

"Naturally. To support Minnesota's football team."

"I root for Green Bay." Not really. She didn't like football at all, but she did love stirring the pot.

"Traitor."

"Huh, would you look at that? We're each spilling our guts, and we've only had four skirmishes."

The game continued over the next hour. She learned that he grew up in a small town outside of Rochester. He was thirty-three years old, just a couple years older than her. His dad was a contractor. His mom a retired roofer. Two of his sisters went into teaching and the third was a professional student supporting herself as a rideshare driver.

Rita spilled that she was an only child. She'd always wanted to be a Disney princess because everyone adored them, and they always got to wear the prettiest clothes and had the coolest hairstyles. Her father, whom she'd adored, died when she was thirteen.

They continued the game, each flipping over their top card.

Both threes!

"War!" they shouted together as each laid two cards face down, and the third up.

Daniel's was a king. "Beat that, will ya?"

She wrinkled her nose as she flipped hers over.

An ace? *Yes!* She pumped both fists.

And he flopped back in his chair but grinned. "Rigged. I swear this game is rigged."

She answered with a shrug. This was really the moment she was waiting for, to dig a little deeper with her questions, and she had two he had to answer.

"What I want to know is, how long have you known Detective Cramer?"

His brows did a barely perceptible lift, but she saw it. So, she was right. He tilted his head back, his eyes flitting back and forth. Doing the math? Or pondering what lie to tell?

"I guess it's been about twenty years. He was about the same age I am now and working on the force. His wife had just left him, taking their two kids with her. He moved into the house next to ours and we bonded. Guess I was the son he rarely got to see, and I suddenly knew someone cooler than my dad."

Whoa. She hadn't expected him to spill that much. "No take backs."

"None wanted. I just gave you a bonus 'cause I'm nice like that."

She snorted. "And I still get my second question."

"Fire away."

He actually had answered a follow-up question in his response, but that meant she could go even deeper now. "Since he inspired you so much, did you ever think of becoming a cop?"

He leaned toward her. "I not only thought of it. I did become a police officer."

Chapter Eight

*Y*ou did?"

Daniel had a feeling this was where the game was headed, so he'd prepared for the question. His answer would be mostly true, and he wanted to curse at Howard for not allowing him to be completely honest. He'd tell all but his return to the force, but even with that omission, he felt like he was telling too much. Would she respect him any longer?

He splayed his hands on the table, hoping to convey honesty. "With Howard as my mentor, how could I not want to become a cop? He was a real-life hero. I wanted to be just like him." He shook his head and chuckled. "I turned out to be too much like him."

"Hey." Rita reached over the short table and covered his hand. "This is just a game, not a therapy session."

"Yeah, I know, but if I'm going to be hanging around here until the garage is done, it seems there are things about me you should know."

"As long as you don't expect me to do the same."

"No expectations." He tugged away his hand and sat back in the chair. "I went to police academy, easily passed the Peace Officer Licensing Exam. Howard helped get me on the Rochester force, but that was too small for me. I wanted to save the world, and how could I do that in a hick town in Minnesota? Eventually, I got a job with the St. Paul Police Department. I worked. Dated a lot. I learned that women loved dating a 'hero.'" He snorted. "I got engaged. She broke it off two weeks before the wedding because I didn't spend enough time with her."

"She knew you were a cop, right?"

"Yeah, but once the glamour wore off, she realized my job took more hours than I had to give to her. And, to be honest, the broken engagement was the best thing for both of us. She's now happily married with a brood of kids."

"I'm still sorry that happened. A broken heart's painful. I know."

"I suppose you do." At least his broken heart hadn't come with concerns for his life, as Rita's had.

"But that doesn't explain why you left the force."

Trying to hide his sigh, he rubbed a hand over his mouth. "Problem is, I didn't learn from that. I worked. Dated more. Got married to a woman whose sister I'd been protecting. She divorced me when her sister was murdered."

Rita gasped.

"Yeah, that's the usual response."

"I'm so sorry. I . . . " She sat there, frozen, her mouth gaping open. "Can I ask, uh, do you mind telling me what happened?"

Not really, but his therapist had told him with each retelling it would get easier, and the truth would eventually break through the lies he'd told himself. "The *CliffsNotes* version is that we thought we'd caught her stalker, and it turned out we had the wrong guy. When we realized the mistake, I was too late getting to her."

"So, it wasn't your fault."

"Depends upon how you look at it. My ex blamed me a

hundred percent. How do you argue with someone who just lost her sister and counted on you to protect her? After that, I questioned my every move, which made me a lousy cop, so I quit. Moved back to Rochester, bought a fixer upper, which I flipped, which led to more houses. People started calling me to fix things—thanks to my parents, I'm sure—and I learned I could make a decent living as a handyman. And there's my life story. More than you wanted to know."

Yet still far from the entire truth.

"You didn't have kids, I assume?"

"That's one thing I'm grateful for. No kids, though I really wanted to be a dad just like mine." He shook his head. "As I said, I took after Howard. I did hear through the grapevine—aka my rideshare-driving sister—that Heather is married again and expecting. She's happy. How can I be bitter about that? And really, she taught me a lesson: never fall in love again."

"That sounds lonely."

He shrugged. "It can be, but I've got loving parents. Good friends. A great church. Even my annoying sisters dote on me. Best of all are my four nieces who I've intentionally spoiled to get back at their moms for terrorizing me when I was little." He allowed a grin with that.

He debated telling more of his story—that he'd been depressed following his divorce and had seen a psychotherapist who helped him work through the illness. But then he'd have to share the rest. That eventually, he was able to return to a job he loved and was good at, despite that hiccup in St. Paul. He still visited a therapist regularly to make sure he didn't relapse. For this job, he needed to be a hundred percent healthy—mentally, physically, and spiritually.

And that meant revealing as much truth as his assignment

allowed. "There is one more thing I need to be honest about." He reached to the small of his back and pulled out his gun. "I carry this. Always."

She blinked, and an array of emotions spread across her face, landing on anger. "This whole time you've worked for me, you've carried a gun?"

"I'm sorry I didn't tell you."

"Wow." She shook her head. "I go from one loser to the next, don't I? If you would have told me at the beginning, I would have said, 'cool.'"

"No, you wouldn't have. Not with what you were going through, it would have scared you away."

She got up and paced her little kitchen. Poured herself a cup of water, sipped half, then tossed the rest down the drain. "You're right." She returned to her seat and sat bolt straight. "But from here on in, I need the truth from you, got it?"

He crossed his heart while begging God for forgiveness. "Got it." The truth was, he was there to protect her, no matter what it cost him. Even the friendship of this woman he was starting to like too much.

Rita fingered the card pile in front of her, which was much larger than the pile in front of Daniel. Unless something drastic happened, she was going to win this war.

But was she, really?

Why was it she kept choosing losers? Guys who were dishonest? Men who used her?

But was Daniel using her? What did he get from her? That was an angle she hadn't figured out yet. His story about once being a cop made sense. And it filled in other blanks about him as well. For now, she'd be on alert. She wouldn't readily trust him as she'd trusted . . . William.

She tapped her card pile. "I think it's time we finish this game and put you out of your misery. Loser treats the other to their favorite snack."

He heaved a breath that seemed to puff away the heaviness that had permeated the room. "What is your favorite snack?"

"Uh-uh. No questions until you win a skirmish."

"Fine. But know that I plan to win back that pile of cards, and you're going down."

"Ha. That's what you think!"

He won the first skirmish—her favorite snack is Pop Rocks. She won the second—his favorite snack is whatever food is in front of him. Typical male. To prove it, she set a bowl of peanuts on the table, which he devoured as they played. Then she put out a jar of pickles. Same result. Followed by the last snack-like item she had in the house, Cap'n Crunch. Not a crumb left.

Which was almost equal to the number of cards he had in front of him. Four, to be exact. One lost war, and he'd be out. It was time to finish this game, find bedding for him, and get some sleep. Admittedly, she liked the idea of a former cop sleeping on her couch. She'd probably rest easier than she had in nearly two months.

"Ready?" She gripped her top card. "You go first."

He flipped his over and groaned.

A three! *Ha!*

Rita folded her hands together and stretched them out in front of herself, cracking her knuckles, then peeked at her top card.

No.

"What is it?"

"Want to place a bet?"

"I don't bet."

She flipped over the card. A three.

"I live another day." Daniel slapped two cards face down on the table, followed by a seven.

Making her sweat. This game could go either way. He wins, he gets an additional four cards, which gives him life. And two additional questions. After her grilling of him, she hated to think of what he'd come up with for her. She certainly wouldn't confess to everything, like he'd done.

She put down one card and looked over at him.

He just smirked.

She laid down another.

"Come on, come on. I need to know if I have to run out and find a bag of Pop Rocks."

Oh, that treat would be good right now.

Closing her eyes, she set the third card face up, then blinked in time to see Daniel doing some stupid victory dance.

"You won a single war, not the entire game."

"I have to take whatever I can get." He rubbed his hands together. "Now, contemplating what juicy questions I should ask you." He waggled his brows.

"Oh brother."

"My sisters used that expression many times around me."

"Are you going to ask or not?"

"Fine. Here we go." He licked his lips, leaned toward her, and spoke in a whispered voice, "What's your favorite color?"

She snort-laughed and slapped a hand over her mouth. "If I ever meet your sisters, I'm going to tell them you earned every bit of harassment they gave you."

"I'm sure I did. Now, answer my question."

"Fine. It's red. Bright red."

"Like your hair."

"Yep."

"And your bedroom."

"Of course."

"And your personality."

"Absolutely." She grinned. "Once, I even colored all my hair red."

"All?"

"Not just random strands."

"I wish I could have seen it."

"I rocked it, you know. Not everyone can."

He laughed and began gathering up the cards. Maybe he forgot about the second question.

If she laid down fast enough, he'd forfeit. New rule. She reached for her top card.

"Uh-uh, not so fast."

Shoot.

"I have one more question coming."

"Your time's running out."

"I didn't realize this was a timed game."

"Five. Four."

"What made your mom kick you out of the house when you were eighteen?"

Rita cringed. Yes, Daniel had spilled his guts, but she hated talking about that part of her past. She'd banished that selfish child ages ago.

"I'm sorry." He raised both hands in the air. "You don't have to answer that. I'm stuffing that question right back in." He made a motion of stuffing his mouth. "Now, my real question is, 'What's your dream job?'"

Should she take the easy way out and answer his second question, or dive in, like he had and confess about her rebel years? Admitting her many indiscretions to her handyman was nuts. She'd already confessed them to God, and He'd washed her clean, so no other confession was necessary, right?

For now, anyway. "Thank you for the mulligan."

"You golf?" How easily he changed the subject.

And she sure appreciated it. "Once, but that's another story."

"For the next time we play this game."

"I think one time is enough."

"You're probably right." He chuckled. "So, tell me about your dream job. Is it still being a princess?"

"No, but you know what would be amazing? Being the person who delivers unexpected gifts and surprises to others. Like you see on TV all the time. Like what talk show hosts do. No catches, just knock on their door and tell them, 'Congratulations, you won food for life, or a new home, a new car or—'"

"Or a home remodel." He smirked.

"Yes. That's it exactly. To be able to feel that love . . . " She stopped herself and closed her eyes. What had her response been when he knocked on the door? Suspicion. And that didn't stop, even now. "That's not what happened, is it?"

He shrugged.

"I'm sorry." She should have met him at the door with a hug and exclamations of "You're my hero!" Which was exactly who he'd turned out to be.

"No need to be sorry. Life circumstances dictate our response to events. You were suspicious, and that was the correct response when I knocked on your door. If you think about it, that's the same response Jesus receives from those who encountered Him, back when He walked the earth and now. We know we're not worthy of His love, of His sacrifice."

"Which makes us question His motives. At least I did."

"You're certainly not alone. When my ex-wife filed for a divorce, I wasn't too happy with God, but He never gave up on me."

"Guess I'll have to think up a new dream job. So, does that mean I have to answer your first question?"

Please say no.

"I think you're good." He got up and gathered the cards. "And I think it's time for me to get some shut-eye. One eye at a time, mind you. I'll be alert to anything out of the ordinary."

"I'll find you some bedding. Sorry about the lumpy couch."

"It's a place to rest my head. But first, I want to do a perimeter check of your house."

"Once a cop?"

"Yep. Always a cop."

She watched him head toward the front door, his head on a constant swivel, taking in everything. Protecting her and asking for nothing in return.

Grace.

She could trust him with her past, couldn't she?

"Daniel?" she said as he reached for the doorknob.

He stopped and turned around. "Is there a problem?"

"No." She stared at her foot drawing invisible shapes in the threadbare carpet, then dared to meet his gaze. "To answer your earlier question, the reason Momma kicked me out was because I'd become a rebel. Messing around. Shoplifting. Disrespecting

111

her, teachers, anyone in authority. She kicked me out because I deserved it."

Warmth, rather than judgment, filled his eyes. "And now you're gracing her with care. That's a beautiful thing."

He smiled, and—oh my—her heart stood still. If she wasn't careful, she could easily fall for her handsome handyman.

What just happened there?

Daniel shuddered as he walked to the back of the house, searching for anything that caught his eye.

Tonight, that had been Rita.

What was wrong with him, anyway? A pretty woman smiles at him, flirts a little, and his heart starts palpitating? Get a grip, Winter!

He needed this walk in the fall air to cool himself back to normal and screw his head on straight. Tomorrow he'd give his therapist a call, set up a session. Tonight, his main focus was Papa Flynn—the snake loved to let things simmer. He'd threaten, then let his target anxiously wait it out while he went deeper into hiding. The threat would escalate, then the potential victim would wait some more. And so on.

With Flynn's son in jail, though, Daniel's gut told him this wait would be shorter. Maybe rushing himself was what would trip up Flynn, and he'd make the mistake that would get him jailed.

As long as no one else was hurt in the process.

Outside, everything checked out, as far as he could tell, so he made the call to Steinbach and Wallace. No signs of trouble their way either.

He sat on the garden bench that had a clear view of the house and backyard and called Howard.

"How's she doing?" Howard asked. No greeting, just right into the issue.

"Holding up. She's more worried about her mom than herself." Daniel watched the light flicker on in her bedroom. "Anything on your end? What did the cameras show?"

"Exactly what we anticipated. Some punk kid looking for a fast buck. Couldn't tell us a thing about the person who mailed the menu to him. All communication was handled with burner phones around the city. Can't even nail down a central location."

"Naturally." Daniel got up and walked across the street to survey the home from there. "Is Wallace all set for tomorrow?"

"If Ms. Dunlap is still insisting on staying there."

"It would take a catastrophe to get her to leave."

"A catastrophe is exactly what I'm afraid of. I hope she doesn't end up regretting her decision."

"She's in good hands. I'll be hanging around a few more weeks to finish up the garage, see if there are any other things to be fixed in the house, and Wallace'll be close during the day," he reiterated to assure himself. "Tonight, I'm staying here."

"I don't need to remind you not to mix business and romance."

"This isn't about that. After the scare tonight, she's jittery. I offered to camp out on the couch."

"As long as that's all it is. Seems to me it was romance that messed you up in St. Paul."

"Is this my team leader or counselor talking?"

"A little of both."

Daniel knew better than to dismiss Howard's thoughts, but St. Paul wasn't going to happen again. "I've been twice-burned. I know how to protect myself near a fire."

"The best option is to avoid a fire."

True. But this assignment made that impossible. "I'll do the best I can."

"I know you will. And know, too, that Marlys and I are covering you with prayer."

"Much appreciated." He ended the call and lifted a prayer of thanks for Howard and his new wife and all the other prayer warriors in his life. With them, how could he fail?

Chapter Nine

*D*aniel knocked on Howard's open door before entering. His mentor looked up and shook his head. Daniel had asked the same question every time he'd stopped by the police station—"Anything new on the Flynn's?"—and, every time, he received the same answer. Something had to give soon.

Problem was, he would no longer be there to protect Rita. He'd built the garage, then had focused on the home's interior, fixing leaky faucets, re-caulking shower tile, widening doors into the bathroom and Glady's bedroom for the eventuality that she'd be in a wheelchair. In the two months he'd been around, the woman had slowly gone downhill.

"Hanging up your toolbelt?" Howard asked while focusing on his computer monitor.

"Guess so." He took a seat opposite Howard. "Isn't there anything else I can do? I hate leaving a case unfinished."

And he'd come to cherish his time spent with Rita and even her mom, who always insisted they were dating. Whatever made her happy and less agitated. Truth was, he was going to miss Rita far more than he should, and that irritated him.

"Your assignment was to protect her. You've done that. Now it's time to move on. Wallace is still there every day. Steinbach and Kenyon are keeping an eye on them from across the street. She'll be safe."

"I know." But it still bugged him that he was no longer the protector.

As if he were God. Sheesh, what an arrogant piece of work he was, thinking that he was the only one who could do the job, forgetting that God was in control. The same mistake he'd made in the big city.

"I'm ready to move on." Which also meant he could reveal the truth to Rita. She wasn't going to be happy. "What have you got for me?"

Howard handed him a file. "Another undercover job. We need you to keep an eye on Lars Ollson and do some digging on him."

Daniel flipped open the file and a white-haired, wrinkled-faced man stared back at him. The guy had to be eighty-five. "He needs protection?"

Howard laughed. "The guy needs to get caught. He's a serial shoplifter who's gone from lifting candy to electronics. Every time we bring him in, his fancy lawyer gets him off with claims of mental instability. But many of those stolen items are suddenly showing up for sale on online marketplaces. I think the geezer knows exactly what he's doing. We need you to catch him in the act."

"Shouldn't be a problem." He slapped the folder shut and stood. "I'll be on it tomorrow." Tonight was reserved for the Dunlaps. He'd been invited over for a Thank You meal. How could he turn that down? He aimed for the door.

"Daniel?"

He looked back.

"It's good to see you on the job. Your folks are pretty proud of you."

"Thanks." He sure hoped they were proud. He'd see them—his sisters and their families—on Thursday. He'd always loved Thanksgiving, but this one was going to be different. Last year had been his first without Heather, and he'd pretty much been a jerk to everyone. No one had complained when he left early. This year, he planned to enjoy the day and show his family he'd banished that jerk forever.

He strode from the station, exchanging holiday greetings as he left. He should arrive at Rita's just in time for supper.

One she'd purchased out of her own earnings.

Talk about being proud.

She'd finished the online coding course and had found a work-from-home job almost immediately. With Wallace there helping with Gladys, Rita was able to work. He sure loved the glow coming from her since she got that job.

He pulled his truck in front of the Dunlap home which was now a ray of sunshine on this block. New paint. New roof. New yard. And a new ramp. The home's value had doubled, he was sure, since he first saw the place. Not that Rita cared about that.

In every decision she made, her mother's well-being was at the forefront. She had no clue how attractive that was. Another reason why it was good for him to move on to a new assignment.

He got out of his pickup into the frigid air and grabbed the homemade lemon cheesecake his mom had sent along for him. He couldn't arrive empty-handed, but he also refused to bring anything he'd made. He wanted to keep friends, not drive them away.

Whistling, he walked up the short sidewalk, then up the ramp he'd built, and rang the working doorbell.

Seconds later, the door flew open and his breath caught in his throat.

Wow.

He swore his eyeballs popped out of the sockets at the sight of Rita with the red, above-the-knee dress that emphasized her figure.

She waved him in. "You approve?" Grinning, she twirled strands of hair that matched the red in her dress and on her lips.

"You look—" His voice squeaked like he was going through puberty again. He hung his coat on the coat tree, taking that moment to clear his throat and jam his eyes back where they belonged. "You look amazing. I didn't realize this was a dress-up occasion." All he'd worn was a pair of jeans and an old sweater.

"I take every opportunity I can to dress up."

"Well, I'm glad you did."

"You're not too bad yourself. You look good without sawdust- and grease-covered jeans."

"Huh. I thought you liked the look."

"I do, but this is much better."

"Is my date here?" Gladys shuffled from the bedroom wearing a shirt that looked like a patchwork-quilt, and a skirt with rainbows dancing across it. Only then did he smell the enticing aromas coming from the kitchen. Seeing Rita had overtaken all his senses.

He walked to Gladys and offered her his arm, as he used to do with his grandma. "Ready for dinner?"

"I am. Where are we dining today?"

"Rita's kitchen."

The woman stiffened and wrinkled her nose. "I had a daughter named Rita. Ungrateful child."

Oh boy. He glanced at Rita, and she shook her head. More often, Gladys was becoming agitated and taking it out on her daughter. That was the norm with this disease, unfortunately.

The easiest person to vent frustrations on was the person they spent the most time with. With Grandma, she'd taken her frustrations out on his mom. Caregiving was a wearying task, but his mom had handled it with incredible grace. But she'd also had backup when things had gotten bad.

With the exception of Officer Wallace hanging around as a pretend caregiver, Rita was alone in this season of life. And now he'd be around even less to deflect attention, so he had to make tonight special.

He led Gladys to the kitchen table, where he seated her and spread a napkin over her lap. Then he whispered to Rita, who was pulling something from the oven, "How can I help?"

"Can you pour beverages? Water for Momma." She nodded toward a cupboard to the right of the sink. "She likes the yellow glass, and be sure to put a lid on it and call it wine."

"At your service." He opened the cupboard door and found a shelf of sippy cups like those his nieces used. He knew Gladys had been spilling a lot. Made sense that this was the solution. He filled the glass with filtered water, capped it, then brought it to the table.

"Your wine, madam." He set the beverage in front of her.

And she giggled. "You're too much, Eldrik."

Eldrik? He shot a glance at Rita, who rolled her eyes as she handed him a serving bowl filled with mixed salad.

Again, she whispered. "Serve it to her or the entire bowl will end up on the floor."

With the salad spoons, he dished a palm-sized amount onto Gladys's plate.

"I'd like cheese too, please."

As if reading her mother's mind, Rita gave him a cheese grater.

"Say when." He turned the handle.

"When what?" Gladys fingered the romaine while wrinkling her nose. "I don't like this."

"Ahh, but it's much better with cheese." He started grating, and she slapped it out of his hands.

"Momma!" Rita's entire body was rigid as she bent and picked up the grater. "I've told you, no throwing food."

Giggling, Gladys dumped the entire contents of her salad bowl on top of Rita's head.

Rita jerked upward, her fists balled and face red. "I. Can't. Do this anymore." She ran from the kitchen, and Daniel fought against the urge to run after her.

"Lord, what do I do?"

He looked around the small but usually tidy kitchen strewn with dirty dishes that evidenced precious time had been spent on making the meal. For Rita's sake, he wasn't going to let it go to waste.

He turned the oven to warm and put the lasagna back inside. Then he cleaned up the mess on the floor and gave Gladys a clean bowl with fresh greens with cheese already grated. She grumbled about not liking it and picked the cheese off the top.

Should he serve her lasagna? Maybe just a small bite-sized piece to see what she did with it. He spooned out a corner of the lasagna and plated it on plastic wear for Gladys. "Dinner is served."

"What is this?" She sniffed at it. "Dog food?"

That plate ended up face down on the floor.

Okay, if that was how she was going to behave, he'd try another tactic. He knew she loved tuna fish and Miracle Whip sandwiches, so that was what she was going to be served.

He whipped together tuna with the salad dressing, spooned

some on bread and cut the sandwich into hors d'oeuvre-sized squares, then put one square on a clean plate. "*Le poisson* for you, madam." He bent as he delivered the plate to the table.

Again, Gladys sniffed at the sandwich. This time, though, her face brightened. "How did you know I wanted fish?" She gobbled up that piece and asked for seconds, along with more white wine.

"As you wish."

A half hour later, the sandwich was eaten, she'd consumed several glasses of "wine" and had shuffled off to bed, claiming all the wine had made her tired.

Talk about tired.

With no sign of Rita, he plopped down on a kitchen chair, then looked at the floor beneath Glady's seat. His work wasn't done yet. How did Rita do this day in and day out and not go crazy? She deserved a night out without worry, without all the work that came with caring for an adult who was regressing as the days went on.

It wouldn't be a date. Just an evening shared between two friends.

But first they had to get through *this* evening.

He scrubbed the floor and the dishes and put everything away, then went to Rita's door and knocked softly, not wanting to disturb Gladys.

No response.

A warning signal went off in his mind. He grabbed his gun as he tried the door.

Locked.

He pounded on the door, no longer caring about bothering Gladys. "Rita. It's Daniel."

More silence.

Please, God, let her be all right.

He jammed his shoulder into the door he'd reinforced. It didn't budge.

He backed a few feet down the hallway and made a run at it.

He threw his body, shoulder first, into the door, and it flew open. He bulldozed into Rita, knocking her onto the floor with him landing on top of her.

"What in the world?" She shoved at him.

And he pushed himself off, trying to slow his breath to normal, his gun still clutched in his hand. "You . . . weren't . . . answering." He sat up and concentrated on normalizing his breath.

"What in tarnation?" Gladys appeared in the doorway, half dressed. *Oh boy.* "If you two are going to fool around, you should do it with the door closed. And quieter. Kids these days." She shuffled away.

Seated on the floor beside him, Rita started giggling.

Daniel couldn't help it. He joined in.

"You should have seen your face when you landed on top of me." Rita wiped tears from her eyes. "Pure horror."

He tucked away his gun. "I thought I'd hurt you. I thought . . . " He breathed in through his nose to the count of eight and let it out just as slowly. "I thought the Flynns got to you."

"And you came to rescue me."

"That had been the plan."

"I was asleep. Dreaming of Bermuda and tanned men with six-packs, and you took me away from that." She smirked and nodded toward the hallway. "And you broke my door."

"Sorry about that." He scratched his head. "All that ran through my head was that Papa Flynn got to you, and I'd never see you again, and honestly . . . " He turned to her and their gazes met. And his lips tingled with wanting. He touched her cheek, wet from happy tears. "Do you mind if I kiss you?"

She looked toward the hallway, where the door hung halfway on the hinges, then got up on her knees, embraced his cheeks between her hands, and feathered her lips across his before backing away, tying his stomach in knots.

He gulped. It was time to leave. Adrenaline rushes made you do stupid, regrettable things.

"You need to go." She got up, arms crossed, and backed into the hallway.

"I know." He followed her into the hallway and looked back at the door. "I'll fix it tomor—"

"I think I can do it on my own." Her arms remained crossed as she walked to the living room.

"You don't have to." He made his way to the front door.

"But your job is done." She stopped by her mother's rocker and turned to him. "You're leaving, and I need to learn to take care of the house on my own."

He remained across the room. "I'll teach you."

She flopped down into the rocker, cradling her face in her hands for a moment before looking toward him. "I'm scared."

That he understood. "You have reason to be. But we—they'll catch the Flynns."

"Not about them, doofus. About me. And you."

He blinked, processing what she said.

Oh.

"I like you, Daniel."

He couldn't stop a smile with that.

"But men just use me."

He resisted taking a step closer to her, wanting to hold her. "I'm sorry that's what others have taught you." What women had taught him. And precisely what he'd show Rita when he admitted he'd been undercover. Oh boy, this was a mess. His new assignment was going to be much easier.

Still, he wasn't going to let it end here. "Go out with me. We'll get Officer Wallace to stay with your mom."

"I don't want to take advantage of her."

"Protecting you and Gladys is her job."

Rita smirked. "Does that mean you'll be protecting me?"

"I won't let anyone get to you." He dared take a single step forward. "How about Saturday, after Thanksgiving."

"Gee, I don't know. I'll have to check my schedule." Which he knew was nearly a hundred percent stay-at-home with her mother.

Which meant on Thanksgiving Day, the two of them would be alone. Not if he could help it. He smiled and took another step forward. "I'd also like both of you to join our family for Thanksgiving."

She snorted. "Um, have you met my mother? She's a bit of a handful to take anywhere."

"And my family's been through it. They'll understand, believe me. And they'll welcome both of you."

"She'll freak out."

"Well, we'll have to come up with a plan to ease that." What would they have done for his grandma? He closed his eyes to shut out the distractions—namely one Rita Dunlap—and thought back to caring for Grandma. Mom had an answer for almost every detour. "I got it." He snapped his fingers and dug out his phone. "Sending you a bunch of pictures of my family, the home, so you can familiarize your mom with everything."

"Really think that'll work?"

"It's worth a shot, right?"

"Are you sure you want us there?" She got up from the chair

and took a step toward him. In this small room, just three steps would put her in his arms.

"I wouldn't make the offer if I didn't mean it."

She took one more step forward.

Now he could smell her perfume. "I'll pick you both up at around eleven."

"You're sweet, you know that?" Another step.

Gulping, he backed away and turned to retrieve his coat.

"Seriously? You're going to break down my door, ask me out, then leave without another kiss?"

He quirked a smile as he put on his coat. "I've been married. I know what kisses lead to."

She laughed and joined him at the door. "Oh, I know what they lead to as well, and as much as part of me wants to go there, it's more important that I wait."

Which, ironically, made her all the more attractive.

"As long as we have that understanding." He zipped up his coat, took her in his arms, and just held her. She fit so perfectly against him. Then he looked down, met her cloudy gaze, and pressed his lips to hers.

She threaded her hands behind his neck and deepened the kiss, overheating his entire body.

Then she released her hands and her lips and backed away, showing him a coy smile. "Just wanted to make sure I'd see you on Thursday."

"Try to keep me away." He left the home and practically floated down the sidewalk. His phone buzzed in his pocket, and he pulled it out.

Officer Steinbach.

"What's up?" He reached his pickup and looked back at the house, realizing with dread that he'd let down his guard.

"Just wanted to remind you that we're watching, listening, and those curtains of hers should be changed. We could see everything through them."

Daniel's face heated. He resisted looking up at the apartment building, showing them what he thought of their spying.

Which was what they were paid to do.

"Jerks," was all he said, then stabbed the End Call button.

Still, the call sobered him. Less than two months into his new job and already he'd broken his personal vow to not fall for someone.

It would kill him if he broke her heart.

But that was exactly what he'd do when he told her she'd been his assignment, that he was still a cop.

Maybe if he made the confession on Thursday, with family around backing him up, she'd find a way to forgive him.

Chapter Ten

Rita stood in front of her bathroom mirror, making sure every hair was in line. Her lips and fingernails were ruby-colored to match her top, and the rest of her makeup was just enough to show that she cared what she looked like. Daniel had usually seen her without makeup and with her hair tucked in a ponytail, so this was a definite improvement. Especially the red she'd dyed her hair's underlayers so that it shone through just enough to make people look closer.

All she cared about was that Daniel looked closer. She licked her lips at the thought.

Two days after his kiss, and Rita could still feel the tingle of his lips on hers. She'd been kissed by a lot of men—far too many—but none had ignited her like Daniel. Robert's, a.k.a., William's, kisses couldn't compare. Funny how, when she'd dated him, she'd convinced herself that didn't matter. That he loved her and was going to make all her problems go away had been her focus.

Daniel never promised to make her problems disappear; rather, he dove in and took care of them, teaching her along the way so she could handle what came up in the future. Just like she'd fixed her own bedroom door. If not for Daniel, she wouldn't have had a clue how.

On top of that, he'd been so amazing with Momma this past Tuesday. Rita had listened at her bedroom door as he gently cared for Momma, treated her like a queen that she certainly wasn't. With Momma taken care of, sleep had come easily for Rita.

But . . .

There was always a *but*. And that was what frightened her.

She put away her makeup and checked on Momma.

Samwise lay by the bed as usual, his tail wagging with contentment. Beside him on the bed was the picture book Rita had created. And Momma? She was pulling on socks over bare legs. Her mom was in shorts. Shorts! In twenty-five-degree weather. *Oh boy*. That meant Rita was in for a battle. If only it were as easy as laying cards down on a pile.

The trick was getting Momma to believe that changing clothes was her own idea.

Rita knocked on Momma's door and walked in. "Don't you look nice! Your favorite, yellow."

Momma looked down and beamed. "I've got a date with Horace today."

Horace? Where did Momma come up with those names? Rita knew just to play along.

"Oh, yes, Horace." She sorted through Momma's closet. Most of the clothes were on the floor. Again. Rita dug through the pile, hoping to find something warm and clean. Hopefully, something that went with Momma's yellow blouse. She found a pair of black slacks that would look lovely with the blouse, and pulled them out. They were a bit wrinkled, but not enough to concern herself with.

She held them up in the air and pretended to study them. "I

remember the last time you went out with Horace, you had on that blouse and these pants and he thought you were the cat's pajamas."

Momma ripped the pants away from Rita. "There they are! I was looking for these."

"You were?"

"Well, of course. Everyone knows these go together. Why did you make me put on shorts?"

"Sorry. My mistake."

"Just don't do it again." Momma wagged her finger.

Rita left the room and mimed bonking her head on the wall. That woman was going to drive her crazy. Bringing her along to the Winter family Thanksgiving celebration was a bad, stupid idea. She'd happily settle for the date with Daniel. He had confirmed Saturday already, with Officer Wallace set to watch Momma. That should be good enough.

The doorbell chimed—she loved the soft tone Daniel had chosen, one that wouldn't aggravate Momma—and Rita hurried to it, beating Samwise by a nose. She'd explain that Momma was being difficult and—

She threw the door open and all thoughts of staying home fled her mind. She thought he'd cleaned up nice for the dinner that didn't happen this past Tuesday, but this left her speechless. A tan blazer covered his button-down, untucked navy shirt that brought out the blue in his eyes. His jeans looked crisp. They were probably new. Even his hair had been combed and gelled.

A single brow shot up. "Like what you see?"

"Oh, yeah."

He stepped inside, petting Samwise, and closed the door behind him. Then he bent down, aiming for her lips.

But she shoved him away. "I just got myself looking perfect, and you want to smudge it?"

His mouth lifted to the right in a lazy smile. "Wouldn't bother me."

"Well it would me." She gave his arm a playful swat. "We're not even officially dating yet—"

"You mean *kissing* doesn't mean we're dating?"

"We haven't been on an official date yet."

"Fine. But I certainly can't kiss anyone I'm not dating. Seems backwards to me."

"Has anyone ever told you you're infuriating?"

"You're about to meet four women who've made that accusation many times."

"And it's those four women I have to look my best for, whether we're dating or not."

Still, he pulled her into his arms and kissed her forehead. "How's that?"

She wrinkled her nose. "On the lips is definitely better."

"Now who's infuriating?"

She giggled. "I better go see if Momma's ready. She dressed in shorts earlier. I think I convinced her to change, but we'll see." Usually, fighting about clothes wasn't a battle she cared to wage, but she really did want to make a good impression on Daniel's family.

Momma's bedroom door was open.

Showcasing her on the bed, with only a bra on.

She groaned and raised her eyes toward Heaven. "Just once, can't things go right?"

"Got a problem?" Daniel snuck up on her, Samwise panting at his side.

She stretched out her arm, stopping him from getting a view of Momma *au natural*. "Believe me, it's not a sight you want to see."

"I'm sorry you have to go through this." He gave her shoulders a gentle squeeze.

"I'm sorry she has to go through this." Rita nodded toward the bedroom. "Momma would be horrified by her behavior."

"So, it's a grace that she can't understand what she's doing."

Contemplating his words, Rita tipped her head to the side and watched Momma attempt to pull on nylons. "You're right. That is grace. I'm going to see if I can help her, then I'll be ready to go, okay?"

"Take whatever time you need. Everyone understands."

Unbidden tears formed in Rita's eyes. She backed from the room and grabbed Daniel's hand. "You're too good to me." Standing on her tippy toes, she pressed a kiss to his cheek, leaving a bright red lips tattoo.

"You deserve to be treated like a princess."

She felt a blush rise to her cheeks. Had she ever blushed around a man? Oh, she was a goner.

Thankfully, Momma didn't resist when Rita offered to help her dress. She even allowed Rita to add a little color to her face. By appearance, her momma looked normal. When was the last time that had happened? Maybe Rita should be more persistent when it came to Momma's appearance, but that was a battle she'd given up on long ago.

At least for today, Momma looked nice. Rita looked fabulous, and Daniel—she peeked out Momma's door as she slipped on her shoes—well, he looked scrumptious. Definitely kissable.

Now all they had to do was get Momma into the pickup without her having a fit, and then make the twenty-mile drive to Daniel's family home.

Oy!

What could go wrong?

Momma sashayed toward Daniel, took his arm, and fluttered her eyelashes.

Oh, brother.

Being the gracious man he was, though, he smiled down at Momma then winked at Rita. "Let's go celebrate."

Maybe the better question was, what couldn't go wrong?

Daniel would have preferred that Rita sit beside him in his pickup, but Gladys insisted she sit by her date. She'd climbed into the cab without having a fit, but would it last?

As he turned the key, he observed Gladys thumbing through pages stapled together. The pictures he'd sent to Rita. Some of his folks and their home. Pics of his sisters and their husbands. Candids of his nieces. He knew Rita would devise a way to share the pictures with her mother and introduce her to his family.

He pulled onto the city street and shot a glance at Rita sharing the backseat with Samwise—well, she had maybe a quarter of it anyway with Samwise taking up far more than his share.

Over the miles, Daniel took every opportunity he could to look back, very much appreciating what he saw. It had been two years since his divorce from Heather. A marriage that lasted three short years, the very definition of failure.

He turned onto a county road that led to his folks' country home, the house he'd grown up in, harassing his older sisters, who gave back the harassment in spades. The home where he'd been taught that marriage is for a lifetime. Yep, he was a failure.

Yet, here God was gracing him with a new relationship. Maybe. This was only the beginning, which was always exciting. Problem was, with his career, the excitement never ended. After what Rita had gone through, would she really want to date a cop?

And there was the real issue.

He sighed, far too loudly, drawing a glimpse at him from Rita. He grinned in the mirror.

She blew back a kiss, which reminded him that he probably still had lipstick on his cheek. Before he got out of the pickup, he'd have to take care of that, or the teasing would start before he entered the home.

To spend the day with Rita, though, would be worth all the ribbing his sisters could dole out.

Today, he had to tell her about his job, what his assignment had been. It couldn't wait. The difficulty would be finding the right time and place to do so.

"There's my folks' home." He nodded toward the white colonial-style house set back from the road. Already he could see his mom's Pomsky jumping around, excited to see him. In spite of himself, Daniel loved the little furball. Goliath had wound his way around Daniel's then-broken heart and helped it heal.

"That's your mom's dog?"

"Goliath."

"Goliath?" Rita giggled.

"Don't let his size fool you. I've seen him take down a full-grown man." Well, okay, that man was him, and he'd been unable to resist lying on the ground and letting Goliath run all over him.

"Do you think he'll get along with Samwise? Maybe we should have left him home."

"Nah, Samwise'll be just fine. Won't you, buddy?" He looked in the mirror at Samwise's slobbery grin.

He pulled his pickup into the Winter parking lot, as Dad called it. Two minivans, one crossover, and one pickup. His entire family was here, oh boy. Mom and Dad knew he was bringing Rita and Gladys, but what would his sisters think of him having a girlfriend again? None of them had been too forgiving toward Heather. They'd probably chastise him for not remaining single.

He'd tried, honestly, he had, but Rita couldn't be ignored.

Neither could Gladys.

"That's Horace's home." She got out of the pickup by herself and strutted toward the house—while Samwise and Goliath checked each other out—like this was her home.

"I can't believe it." Rita hovered by the pickup. "That was way too easy. I keep waiting for the meltdown."

"You prepared her well." He gestured to the photo book on the front seat.

"That's all she's looked at for the past couple of days. Kept telling me that's where she grew up. I never saw the place, but I'm guessing it's similar to this."

"It's a common colonial style home, so could be."

"You know." Rita looped her arms around Daniel's back and looked up at him. "Maybe we should leave Momma here, and you and I take off."

He laughed and shrugged out of her hug then grabbed a couple bags of chips from the back, his contribution for the day. The family knew not to ask him to bring a meal item anymore. They wanted their food warm and on time. "As fun as that sounds, you don't want to miss a Winter Thanksgiving." He held out his gloved hand.

For a second she hesitated, then grasped it.

It felt right, her gloved hand in his, and he wanted to show her off. Sure, he'd take some ribbing from his sisters, but they'd get over it and love Rita as much as he was beginning to.

Side by side, they walked toward the house. Any second now, he expected someone to burst outside and give him the third degree. But chances were, they'd already begun eating. Someday they'd learn that he was perpetually late, unless it was work related, and tell him a meal time half an hour early, so he'd arrive on time.

He followed Rita up the porch steps and held the door open for her. Again, she hesitated.

"You go in first." Rita motioned toward the doorway.

"You scared?"

"Terrified."

"Of what your mom's doing?"

"I'd forgotten about her." She pushed him forward.

He stepped inside the large foyer, with Rita right behind him. He hung both coats on pegs on the wall and placed their footwear alongside a mess of other shoes and boots. No wonder she was terrified. His family wasn't large, but compared to hers, it was dauntingly huge.

"Ready?" He whispered.

She inhaled a breath and blew it out. "Let's get it over with."

Leaving the bags of chips in the entry, he took her hand and led her down the hallway toward the doorway leading into the dining hall, as his mother called it. When they'd built this home, she'd insisted on having a dining room big enough to seat twenty people. That allowed for the four kids, their four spouses, and two children per family. Two of his sisters had complied. He was trying. His other sister was having too much fun with her singleness, and he worried about that. So did his folks.

Mimicking Rita's inhale, they stepped inside the doorway, his hand still in hers. He gulped as heads turned their way, all except Gladys who'd made herself at home at the table while others carried in food from the kitchen.

All his siblings' eyes grew wide. Then Carrie and Ginny shook their heads. Stephenie gave him the thumbs-up.

No surprise there.

His mom came through the doorway from the kitchen, a platter of turkey in her hands, and her face lit up. "Daniel! You're early."

Well, not really. More like just in time.

She set the platter on the table then rushed to hug him, with Dad right behind her. But his nieces beat them all, tackling his knees with the most loving hugs ever. He knelt and did his best to wrap all four in a group hug.

As usual, Mom played the role of hostess to perfection. "Welcome, Rita. Daniel's told us much about you and your mother."

"He has?"

He felt Rita's gaze pierce him from above, and his face heated. He released his nieces and stood. "I have been working at your house the last couple of months."

"True." She gave his hand a quick squeeze. To his parents, she said, "Thank you for welcoming me and Momma."

"Of course." His mom braced her arm around Rita's back and led her to the dining table. "I applaud the care you're giving your mother. It's not an easy task."

"Spoken by someone who performed caregiving with abundant grace." Dad kissed Mom on the cheek.

That was the kind of love Daniel wanted to have someday.

"That's my date," Gladys said, and forked a piece of turkey off the platter.

"Guess that's our signal to sit." Dad took his place, not at the head of the table. He and Mom always preferred the side, where they were among the family rather than presiding over it. The rest of the family followed suit. His brothers-in-law settled their daughters and held chairs for his sisters, each demonstrating how to love on each other.

Taking their cue, Daniel held out the chair for Rita and helped guide it in when she sat.

And then they all gave thanks for their abundant blessings.

Platters and bowls of food were passed his way, and soon his plate was overflowing with food, all mixing together, and he topped it off with gravy. Man, he loved Thanksgiving.

Rita took small portions that didn't touch. Huh. That was something new he'd learned about her.

"How'd the two of you meet?" Carrie asked. As the oldest sibling, she always took charge.

He didn't like telling the lies that were about to come from his mouth, but until he got Rita alone this afternoon, he had to maintain cover. "Gladys won a contest, an extreme handyman makeover. I was hired as the handyman to fix up the place." He didn't miss his mom's pinched smile—she knew the truth. One more way to disappoint his family.

"And I'm Momma's caregiver, so I was there all the time." Rita looked up at Daniel. "In a way, he was my protector in a tough time."

At least that was the truth.

"Rita's a full-time caregiver." Mom explained to the family, pride beaming through her voice.

Rita shrugged in response.

"Which is no wonder why Daniel likes you." Mom smiled at him, affirming his decision to bring Rita and Gladys along. "Nothing is more tasking than caring for an ill parent, and to do it full time is heroic."

Now that made Daniel proud. He took Rita's hand, raised it to his mouth, and kissed it. "That's a good word to describe you: heroic." He swore he could feel his sisters roll their eyes. Tough. Seeing Rita's cheeks redden enough to match her lips was worth it.

A few more questions were tossed toward Daniel and Rita, then suddenly they were old news and conversation continued as normal. Football. Christmas. Needling Stephenie about settling down. Dad's new housing project. Mom's retirement from roofing. The most exciting news was that two of his nieces were potty-trained. Which meant he would now be up for babysitting duty.

"When do you start your new assignment?" Stephenie asked him.

He shot her a look and a discreet, he hoped, chopping motion by his neck.

"Um, I mean, new project."

"Yesterday." He focused on his food, hoping Rita didn't catch his sister's slip-up. "For an elderly man."

"Oh? You didn't tell me about that." Was there an edge in Rita's voice?

He started to sweat. "I guess—"

"What is this?" Gladys threw a pickled beet onto the floor.

He'd never been so happy for one of her tantrums.

"I'm sorry you don't care for them." His mom took Gladys's plate and slid the beets onto her own. "I see you loved the mashed potatoes."

"And the butter. And the gravy. Lots of gravy."

Mom followed Gladys's lead. "You can have as much gravy as you like."

Two crises averted. Whew. Hopefully, Rita would forget that

conversation thread.

She seemed to, as all too quickly the food was devoured, and the table was cleared. Since they had been the last to arrive, he and Rita got dish duty, a rule his sisters had made up years ago to get out of cleanup. Someday he'd show them and arrive on time or even early and beat them.

Not that he minded having the quiet time with Rita, with her momma occupied by his mom and dad.

"I love your family." Rita handed him a clean china plate which he wiped dry.

"Even with the inquisition?" He set the plate on a stack of others.

"That wasn't so bad." She scrubbed at a small spot on the next plate. "I can tell they love you and want the best for you. It makes sense they want to check me out. They don't want to see you hurt again."

"I get it, but that choice is up to me, and I like you, a whole lot." He bent and stole a kiss.

She giggled in response.

"Way to make me feel manly."

She giggled again. "Well, it's just that you never wiped off my lipstick from earlier."

"What?" He ran to the bathroom down the hallway, and sure enough, her lips were still tattooed to his cheek. Oh, man. His sisters and brothers-in-law were probably having a good chuckle at his expense. He scrubbed it off and returned to the kitchen. "Better?"

She shrugged. "I rather liked it there."

He bent close to her and whispered. "When we're done here, we'll go for a walk and I'll gladly let you put it back."

"Hmm." She tapped her chin. "I'll have to think about that."

He stole another kiss. "Think on that."

"That was a tease."

"I know." He grinned.

Washing dishes took another half hour, and they were finally ready to head outside. But for Daniel the time passed too quickly. In just a short while, he'd be telling her the truth about his job, and then he'd know if their relationship was over before it started.

Rita dressed in her winter coat and gloves, wrapped her red-knitted scarf around her neck, and topped her head with a matching stocking cap. Thank goodness the snow that had fallen this past weekend had mostly melted. Trudging through snow wasn't her idea of fun. They snuck out of the house before Momma noticed them—though she was enjoying being the center of attention. Daniel's parents were amazing with her, although she'd now started to flirt with Daniel's dad, who'd quickly removed himself from her vision.

They stepped outside and were nearly assaulted by the two dogs. She'd never seen Samwise so happy. All this space to run had to be an amusement park for him, and having a friend to share it with made it even better.

"Should we bring them with us?" She bent to pet Goliath, and Samwise nosed his way beneath her hand. "Hey buddy, you have to share."

"Goliath should probably go in. He's older and won't like the long hike." He picked up the dog. "Be right back."

"Guess it's just the three of us then, huh, boy." She rubbed Samwise's face between her hands, and he licked her in return.

"Hey, that's my girl, mister."

His girl. Rita liked the sound of that.

He handed her an insulated mug. "Mom's homemade hot cocoa. You'll never use store bought again."

She sipped, and her eyes rolled back in her head. "This is heavenly."

"Right? Just like walking with you."

"And that was corny."

He guffawed at that.

"By the way." She leaned into him. "Andrea said thank you—"

"Andrea?"

"Wallace. My—" She made air quotes. "—hired help."

"Ahhh." Her in-home police protector.

"Anyway, she said 'thank you for the day off.' She gets to spend Thanksgiving with her son now."

"Wallace has a son?"

"You say that like you know her."

"I know a lot of cops in the area."

"Hmmm." Guess that made sense, him being an ex-cop. For the next half hour or so, they walked. And talked. And just listened to nature. She could very easily get used to this. But this was a fairy tale. She still had Momma to care for. Papa Flynn was still on the loose. When she returned home tonight, Daniel would deliver her right back into her life, jailed within the walls of her momma's home.

"Something wrong?" He looped his arm around hers.

"Just thinking."

"Care to share?"

Not today. She shook her head. Maybe real life wasn't a fairy tale, but she could pretend for the day.

They walked around a pole shed near the house, and she

spotted a fire pit surrounded with wooden benches. Probably made by Daniel and his father. A line of trees cut between the shed and house, giving them privacy.

"Have a seat. I'll get this going."

Minutes later, he had a fire blazing, and they cuddled together, drinking their hot cocoa, sharing kisses, with Samwise content at their feet. Yep, fairy tale.

He kissed her long and sweet then pulled back, resting his forehead on hers. "I need to tell you something."

She stiffened, and pulled away, not liking his tone. Was her fairy-tale afternoon about to burn?

She stared at the fire as Daniel began his story after Heather left him. How he'd moved back to the Rochester area and fallen into a deep depression. For over a year, he'd seen a therapist.

"Why didn't you tell me this?"

"Because it doesn't end there. I was given the okay to return to work."

"As a handyman." She said, even though her gut warned that wasn't the right answer.

"To the force. I was hired on by the Rochester Police Department as a detective. I do undercover work."

No.

The shakes began then as she tugged away from Daniel's embrace.

"I was hired to protect you." *And to spy on you.* That she didn't need to know.

She balled her fists. "Momma didn't win a contest."

"No, she didn't."

Her jaw tightened. "You're not really a handyman."

"Well, I am, but that wasn't my primary job with you."

Her teeth chattered and she hugged herself. "How dare you

lie to me!"

"I didn't have a choice. It was my job."

"Am I still your job? Is dating me part of your assignment?" She spat the word at him.

"No, it's—"

She poked him in the chest. "You said long ago you were done with romance. I should have figured it out that I was being played." She got up and tossed the rest of her cocoa onto the fire. The fire hissed back. "I am such a chump."

"It's not that way, Rita." He got up and walked toward her.

She held out her hand, giving him the stop sign. "You lied to me from the beginning, just like every other jerk I've dated."

"What I feel for you isn't a lie."

She snorted, and stomped away from him, away from the house, across a field that had remnants of corn stalks.

"Where are you going?" he called after her.

"Wherever you're not." Oh, she wanted to give him the one-finger salute, but she resisted. She didn't want to hurt God, but she wasn't very thrilled with the male species He'd created.

"Samwise, stay with her."

The dog bounded to her side. This was unconditional love. Mankind had a whole lot to learn from dogs.

Her body trembled from once again being betrayed, lied to, used. As much as tears wanted to fall, she refused to shed one more over a man.

With shaky fingers, she reached for the phone in her pocket. She'd find a road and call a ride share. Maybe Stephenie would pick her up. She seemed to have as much time for men as Rita did. She was done with men, once and for all. All they did was lie to her and hurt her.

Chapter Eleven

For the next hour, Daniel sat on the bench alone, waiting, processing, praying. Watching Rita from afar. She'd trudged into the woods that were blanketed with unmelted snow and sat on a fallen tree. Her red hat and scarf stood out well against the snow cover, Samwise sticking by her side. She may not want to see him now, but no way was he going to let down his guard and lose her from his sight.

He'd mucked this one up good. Before Rita, he'd convinced himself he wasn't meant to fall in love. No, he wasn't "in love" with Rita, it was too fast for that, but he did care for her deeply and was eager to see where the road took them.

"You okay, son?"

Dad.

Daniel shook his head.

"Let me guess, you told her the truth."

"You say that like I've intentionally lied to her."

Dad sat beside him. "Haven't you?"

"Yes, but I had no choice. That's my job, Dad, and it reeks. What's God going to say when I meet Him at the pearly gates? Everyone wants to hear, 'Well done.' Is that what He's going to say to me?"

Dad sighed. "You're in a tough spot. I can't pretend to speak for God, but I do know He looks at your heart, and that's in the right place. From what I've heard, you went over and above your assignment at their home. Treated Gladys like a queen. Used your own savings to finance projects."

"Who told you that?"

"Howard and I still talk. He speaks highly of you and was concerned for you."

"Guess he had reason to be." Daniel kicked at the browning grass. "I don't want to lose her, Dad, but I don't think she'll ever trust me again, much less any man."

"Trust in people is a tricky thing."

"Tell me about it."

"But do you trust God?"

Oh, it was so like Dad to bring up the tough issues. "Of course, I do." But did he?

Dad nodded toward the woods, toward the patches of red standing out amidst the snow. "Trusting God means trusting Him with the results even if they're not what you want."

"I . . . " He almost said he did, but that would be a lie. He wanted what he wanted whether that was in God's plan or not. "I have a lot of work to do in that area."

"We all do." Dad slapped his back. "You're not alone, son. What do you think you should do next?"

"That's easy. I need to pray." Keeping watch over Rita, he prayed with his father, giving Rita—her protection and her heart—up to God. And he prayed he'd resist the temptation to snatch back control. That was the hardest part, because he liked, too much, being in control.

"I need to give her space." His first step in letting go.

"That's a start."

A start . . .

"Maybe that's what I should do. Start over at the beginning, lay all my cards out so we don't have any more skirmishes."

Dad laughed. "Oh, there'll always be skirmishes between two people who love and care for each other. It's up to you to determine if those skirmishes refine or ruin your relationship."

"Like me and Heather."

Dad nodded.

Daniel stood, planning to go to her and bring her and Gladys home. No strings attached. "Wish me luck."

"How about I pray for you first?" And then Dad's hand was on Daniel's shoulder. "Heavenly Father, You alone know the plans mapped out for Daniel and Rita. Please restore what has been broken between them and guide their footsteps. Help them to trust You for whatever the outcome might be."

With the prayer repeating in Daniel's head, his phone rang.

He looked at the I.D. Officer Wallace? Oh no. He stabbed Answer. "This is Winter."

"We got him."

What? "Him?"

"Flynn. Papa Flynn. We got him." Her voice shook with excitement.

Daniel fell back on the bench, and immeasurable relief flooded through him. "Tell me about it."

Silence.

"Wallace?"

"Sorry. Just composing myself. The dirtbag was doing ninety on a county road. The county sheriff stopped him and realized he hit pay dirt."

"Wow." Daniel couldn't believe Flynn had been that careless. "Thanks for the good news. Rita will be ecstatic."

"That she will. So, you two gonna shack up then?"

"What? Seriously?" Sometimes he hated cop talk. "Thanks for the update." Shaking his head, he ended the call.

"Good news?" Dad asked.

Daniel nodded. "The best. We caught him." He closed his eyes, raised his hands, and gave thanks. God was good.

Now to share the news with Rita. "She may not want to see me, but she'll like this news." He looked back at the woods, his gaze landing on the red scarf and hat, realizing that once Wallace delivered the news, he'd taken his eyes off Rita. For the first time in months, he could relax.

A dog barked in the distance. Daniel looked beyond Rita then saw Samwise bolting from the woods, toward him.

Alone.

Daniel gulped and fear slithered up his spine.

He ran toward the dog, and Samwise barreled into him. He remained standing, looking into the woods at the hat and scarf. Warning signals went off in his brain, and he pulled out his revolver.

"What's wrong?" Dad.

"Go back to the house. Now. Get everyone inside. Lock it. Set the alarm."

"But—"

"Now!"

His dad didn't argue again, but hustled back to the house as Daniel pulled out his phone and called Howard while running toward Rita.

"What's up?" He answered after one ring.

"Is Papa Flynn in custody?"

"Who told you that?"

"Wallace."

Howard cursed. "He got to her."

Daniel reached the edge of the woods and his blood ran cold. Rita's hat and scarf hung on a tree with no sign of her. Footprints in the snow led from the woods to the county road.

"I need the team out here ASAP."

"Don't go alone, Daniel."

"I don't have a choice." Knowing Flynn's past, Rita might not have much time.

"What did Wallace tell you?" Howard asked.

Daniel repeated the conversation, except for the shacking up part, and realized how bizarre that had been. "I think she left us clues."

With Samwise at his side, he started walking the road. County Road 90.

Shacking up . . . He closed his eyes and pictured a number of places he and his buddies had explored years ago. Most were gone now, but there was one . . .

"I think I know where she is." He gave directions and started running down the road.

His phone beeped his text tone.

Rita!

He pulled up the text and his blood froze.

– She says you're always late.

That's too bad. –

Chapter Twelve

His heart pumping faster than Samwise could run, Daniel got on the phone with Howard.

"He's got her." He read the text. "Can you trace it?"

"Didn't you put a tracker on her phone?"

"I had, but I removed it when my assignment ended." That'd teach him for being conscientious. A good cop wouldn't have cared about the morality of tracking her once his assignment ended, because until Papa Flynn was behind bars, she was still in danger. What kind of a cop was he anyway? Like with Heather's sister, he'd let down his guard, and whoosh, the bad guy had swept in.

"Stop it, Daniel. I know what you're thinking. You're a good cop."

Muffled voices came over the line. "One second."

"I don't have . . . " Daniel cut himself off. Running blindly and on emotion would only hurt Rita.

"I have more bad news for you," Howard said.

Daniel jerked to a stop, breathing hard. How could it be worse than this?

"William escaped from jail."

"What? How?"

"Wallace was busy today."

Daniel held back a curse, realizing Rita wasn't the only one in danger. "Make sure Wallace's son is safe."

"Already on it."

"I gotta go. You know where the old Hartzler shack is? I think that's where she is."

"Be careful, Daniel. You'll likely be facing down two Flynns and not just one. Wait for us. We're only fifteen minutes out."

"Not happening. You heard his text. I'm not going to be late again." One Flynn was bad enough, but two?

Besides, if she was where he imagined she was, getting a vehicle there wasn't going to be easy and would take longer than Howard thought.

"Daniel—"

He cut short the call. Running into a situation solo was never a smart thing, but delaying could be deadly.

There was one thing he could do first, though.

Pray. And then he wouldn't be going in alone. This was in God's hands, and Daniel had to trust the results to Him.

He remained in prayer as he ran down the road, across a bumpy field, and through thick copses of trees that slapped his face. The dilapidated house loomed before him, like in a scene from a horror movie. Paint had chipped off years ago, the roof had caved in, and all the windows were shattered. He'd done much of that shattering with his buddies way back when. He also knew the layout of the home, having explored it many times.

If Flynn thought he had the advantage, he was sorely mistaken.

Samwise remained quietly at his side as he crept toward the house, doing his best to avoid fallen branches. At the edge of the woods, he stopped. Listened. Observed.

No lights. No sounds. But he could tell by the indentations in the ground that a vehicle had passed through recently. His gaze followed the tracks. There. On the other side of the house sat an old pickup. Staying in the shadows of the woods, he walked the perimeter of the home to get a look at the truck.

He edged up to it, peeked inside. Empty. Felt the hood. Warm. Odds had it, she was inside the house. He texted the plate number to Howard, but had no doubts that it was stolen.

A text came right back from Howard.

– Stolen –

Duh.

– Five minutes out –

Too long.

Daniel looked for a way in that would hide him.

The old cellar at the back of the house.

Using the trees as cover, he slunk around the house, keeping his gaze on it, his ears open to noises not heard in nature. The cellar doors were bashed in. He should be able to squeeze through.

Bending low, he hurried across the weed-infested yard to the cellar entry. It was too narrow, so he had to raise a door slightly. It creaked.

He stilled.

Listened.

Silence.

Breathe, Daniel, Breathe.

He and Samwise slid beneath the door and then he slowly

closed it above his head. He stood unmoving for a moment, his eyes adjusting to the darkness.

Samwise nudged his hand, assuring Daniel.

If he remembered correctly, the stairs to the main floor of the two-story home were just ahead. He didn't dare turn on his phone light, afraid to give away his position, so he felt his way through the basement, one baby step at a time. When they used to explore this place, the cellar had been empty, but now someone was using it for storage. He had little doubt it was for something else illegal.

He searched the floor with his feet, the air with his hands.

A railing? He grasped it and shuffled a foot forward.

Steps.

Thank you, Jesus.

He placed one foot on the stairs and tested for firmness. It should hold his weight. He tested the next. Fine. The third.

He crashed through to his knee and gasped.

"Daniel!"

Rita!

"Ah, so you've arrived," a Southern voice drawled from above, sending a chill through Daniel. "Come on up, boy, before you're late."

"Where are you?" Daniel flipped on his phone's flashlight as he tugged his leg free. He moved his foot around. A little blood, but no broken bones.

"We're up in the bedroom, son. My boy was planning to marry her, but you ruined that."

"Don't hurt her. I'm coming."

"Better hurry, boy. Don't be late."

Hurry. Right. Up steps that were half missing and rotted. Thank God for long legs that stretched from one step, over rotted ones, to the top. He pulled himself up, panting. Then he zigzagged across the half-there first floor to the stairs leading to the second floor.

"I'm coming," he yelled up the stairs.

"Time's about up. Don't want to be late."

Not caring about the broken steps, he leapt up them two at a time. Some gave way as he pushed off.

He made it. Now, which bedroom?

A yelp sounded behind him. Samwise? He looked back—the dog's only front leg was caught in a broken floorboard.

Daniel didn't have time to go down and help, so he inched forward on his own, all senses on alert.

Flynn had mentioned a wedding, so likely the largest room. What kind of game were the Flynns playing? Were they staging a wedding? His veins iced at the thought.

Still, he wiped sweat from his face as he slid along the wall, his gun going first, his gaze never stopping.

He came to the bedroom and spun inside, gun first.

Its aim landed on Rita.

She was tied to a three-legged chair balancing on a two-by-six that spanned a hole leading all the way to the concrete floor of the cellar. The only thing keeping the chair steady was Papa Flynn's hand on the chair back.

Daniel scanned the room. Where was William? He kept his ears open so the son couldn't creep up behind him.

"Let her go." Daniel finally broke the silence, keeping his voice calm, which wasn't at all what he felt inside. "You've got me."

The man roared with laughter. "Do you know how many times I've heard that line, boy?"

Daniel didn't answer.

Flynn tipped the chair slightly, and Rita screamed. "Do you

know how many times that line has worked? And don't feed me the line that if I let her go free, you'll give me a head start. We both know that isn't happening."

"What do you want, Flynn?" Daniel took a baby step forward.

"I don't like loose ends, boy, and that's you and the young lady here. Her momma's crazy, so she gets to live."

Daniel took another step and heard something behind him or below. Please let it be Samwise or Howard and not William.

"Uh, uh, uh. You stay right there." Flynn tipped Rita's chair some more then looked down at her. "Did my boy tell you I liked playing games?"

"Pops, don't do it."

"Robert?" Rita's chair teetered and she screamed.

"What are you doing here, boy? Who let you out of prison?"

Papa Flynn didn't know!

How could Daniel use that to his advantage?

"Don't you dare hurt her." William's cold tone toward his father sent a chill down Daniel's spine.

"Come on, son, she can put me in prison. You don't want that."

"No, but I don't want her hurt either."

With each verbal volley between father and son, Daniel stepped out of the line of fire between the two and closer to Rita.

"Put that gun away before you hurt yourself." Papa swept a hand in front of himself, his grip loosening on the chair.

Rita's fear-filled gaze met Daniel's.

"You let her go, I put down my gun." William's voice was flinty.

"I raised you to respect me." Papa Flynn's was no less strong.

"By teaching me how to hurt women?" William's voice raised. "No, I can never respect that."

"Now, son, listen. I'm sorry about your last girlfriend, but she was collateral damage."

William flung a curse at his father.

Daniel inched closer. Almost in arm's distance.

"Free her. Now."

"I can't do that, son."

A boom blasted behind Daniel's ear.

Papa Flynn released the chair and fell backward, crashing through the floorboards, thumping way below.

Rita's chair wobbled. Tipped.

Daniel dove, dropping his gun, caught a chair leg. "Hang on, Rita, hang on."

It began slipping.

No!

He gripped both hands on the leg but couldn't get leverage.

And then William was lying at his side, helping pull up the chair. Dragging Rita and the chair to firmer ground.

William peeked through the hole, and sat back, tears in his eyes. "I just wanted to scare him; I didn't want to kill him."

Daniel looked below, then to the wall behind where Papa Flynn had stood. A bullet hole gave evidence that William hadn't shot his father.

He nodded to the hole. "You did what you had to." Daniel worked at the knotted ropes holding Rita to the chair.

"I'm sorry. For everything." His voice shaking, William helped free the knots. "I wanted to break free from the family business, but didn't know how. And now—"

Sirens sounded outside the house.

"I have to go." William got up and dried his face with his arm.

"Don't." Daniel felt in the small of his back for his gun, then realized it was probably lying alongside Papa Flynn. He'd left his secondary revolver at home to appease his oldest sister who wasn't fond of him carrying weapons around her children. Another hard lesson learned. But he still had some tricks up his sleeve. "Turn yourself in, William. With your testimony, things'll go easier on you."

"Yeah, right." He laughed. "I know lawyer-speak, and I'm not falling for that. I've done too much to be forgiven."

"Okay, maybe you're right." Daniel tried stalling. "But that's earthly justice. God's justice is different. Jesus already paid the penalty and is ready to forgive anyone who asks, regardless of what we've done."

"I want to believe that." William stepped toward the door, then ran out.

Daniel didn't have the heart to chase after him. Maybe Howard would catch him. Maybe not. All he knew was that today, William had saved both his and Rita's lives, and for that he was grateful and would offer him mercy, if given the choice.

"You were right on time." Rita's voice couldn't have sounded sweeter.

He looked up and smiled at her. "I was afraid I wouldn't be."

Samwise ran into the room and started licking Rita.

She threw her arms around his neck and nodded at Daniel's shin. "Are you okay?"

Blood soaked his jeans, and he noticed the first twinge of pain. He winced. "Nothing stitches won't fix." He finally freed the last knot, and Rita escaped from the chair, falling into his arms.

"The more important question is, are you okay?" He wiped aside her bangs, and then sat back to examine her arms, legs, body.

"He didn't hurt me."

Really? Maybe not physically, but this incident was going to carry emotional scars. He wasn't the only one who'd be talking to a therapist. But she would be fine. He'd make sure of it.

A bunch of banging, like boards crashing, sounded below. And then he saw the glow of light coming from the hole Flynn had disappeared into.

"Daniel, you up there?" Howard.

"Yeah. With Rita and Samwise. We're good."

"Better than Papa Flynn here. Looks like he won't be selling any more drugs."

"You catch William?"

"He was here?"

"He took care of his dad, then ran off on foot. When you catch him, go easy on him, okay?"

"Whatever you say." Howard motioned to men in the cellar.

Daniel looked to Rita. "Ready to go?"

She nodded. "Thanks for rescuing me."

"Does that mean you'll forgive me?" He searched her eyes. All he saw was sadness.

"I can't answer that right now."

"That's fine." He stood, and pain shot up his leg. Pain was good. It reminded you that all was not right, but broken things could be fixed.

And he had every intention of fixing this relationship.

He prayed she'd want that as well.

They hobbled their way down the half-there steps.

On the main floor, one officer took Rita off to the side for questioning, and Daniel joined Howard outside. With Samwise.

Daniel knelt beside the dog and checked out his front leg. Didn't appear to be hurt, but he'd still have a vet check him out.

"You should have that looked at." Howard pointed at Daniel's shin.

"I will. Just wanted to check in with you first. Flynn's dead?"

"Very."

Daniel heaved a sigh. The death of a criminal never gave him satisfaction. He always wondered what that person could have accomplished had they used their gifts for good. What a waste.

"And just got word, they caught William too." They walked—Daniel limped—toward Howard's unmarked car. "He didn't put up a fight."

"Hopefully, this will be a wake-up call for him. Really, he's the one who saved Rita." Without William there, Rita undoubtedly would have met the same fate as Papa Flynn.

"How does it feel now, being back on the force, your first case solved?"

Daniel looked toward the house, where Rita sat beside a female officer. "Like crap."

"You did your job. You protected her, we got the head of the Flynn clan and the second in command. Without them, the network will crumble. You did good."

"Yeah." He kicked at the ground. "But at what cost?"

Howard leaned against his vehicle, crossing one ankle over the other, while observing the action around the ramshackle house. "One thing my wife's told me is that real love always costs the giver, but should never cost the receiver. Look at Jesus. He paid the death penalty each of us earned."

"Yeah, well, that's the problem. She paid a big price with my charade. She doesn't trust me, and I can't blame her."

"You did your job."

"Well, my job stinks."

"Sounds like you're giving up."

"I'm not quitting."

"Not your job, numbskull." He nodded toward Rita. "You

were doing your job. You did it well, and we got the results we'd hoped for. But now that assignment is over, and you get a fresh start. The question is, are you going to take it?"

Daniel glanced at the house, and his gaze collided with Rita's.

Too quickly, she looked away.

A new start. He could do that.

The problem was, he doubted he'd like her response.

He may have caught the criminal, but it had cost him Rita's heart.

Chapter Thirteen

Had it only been a week since Thanksgiving?

Rita stared out the front window of her momma's home. She was free at last. No Daniel hanging around. No Officer Wallace pretending to be a caregiver while protecting her. She still shivered at the memory of Flynn abducting her from the side of the road.

Why warning bells hadn't sounded when she'd climbed into that old pickup, she didn't know. By the time she'd realized Papa Flynn was behind the wheel, it was too late. In her anger, she'd let down her guard.

It still saddened her that Andrea Wallace, someone Rita had thought of as a friend, was responsible for freeing William and distracting Daniel. But people will go to extreme measures when their child is threatened. Thankfully, both Andrea and her son were safe, although she'd been suspended from the force for her actions.

Problem was this place now felt quiet and lonely. At least with people around, she'd had someone sane to talk to. Someone who could hold an intelligent conversation.

"What are you looking for?" Momma waddled into the room wearing her favorite banana-colored outfit.

"Just looking."

"If you see my date coming, let me know." She sat in her rocker, grabbed the remote, and flicked on the television to watch the same shows over and over again.

Rita would go to her bedroom, sit at her computer, and stare at medical records for much of the day. She felt as if she were caught with Bill Murray in *Groundhog Day*. Every day looked the same.

Being in danger was almost better than this. Instead of having a threat loom over her, now she was trapped in a house without love.

At least Daniel had cared for her.

And deceived me. Don't forget that.

She plodded to the kitchen and looked through the cupboards and fridge, then decided to throw together some soup. Momma wouldn't eat it. Tuna fish sandwiches for her.

The doorbell rang, and Rita stiffened up.

You're safe. Papa Flynn's dead. William's in jail.

She hurried to the door and checked the peephole.

Daniel?

She tamped down her excitement at seeing him. She had to detach herself from him and find someone who didn't cost her trust. Didn't matter that he had just been doing his job.

Did it?

Nope. No doubt.

She threw open the door. "What are you doing here?" Wow, that was polite.

"Just wanted to bring you this." He handed her a business card, just like the one he'd handed her when they first met. Winter Handyman Services, LLC.

"And what am I supposed to do with this?"

"Turn it over."

She did, and read what he'd written on the back. "Free services for life." She flipped it over and back again. "I don't get it."

"Just what it says. You need a handyman, for anything, give me a call. No charge. Ever."

She crumpled up the card in her hand. "I won't be bought."

"I have no expectations, Rita." He splayed his hands. "I just want to do this for you."

"Fine. Whatever."

"I'll see you around." He nodded, turned, and walked away.

"Was that my date?" Momma snuck up behind Rita.

"No. Just a salesman." She brought the card to the kitchen, ripped it up, and threw the scraps in the trash can. She had no intention of using his "free" services. No expectations. *Ha!* She knew better than that.

Rita pulled herself out of bed, made breakfast, made sure Momma was up and settled, then stared at her computer for hours. Yep. *Groundhog Day.*

How could she mix things up, make the day more colorful? From her laptop, she stared upward, and her gaze landed on the calendar. December. Christmas!

What was wrong with her? She didn't even have her Christmas tree up. Momma must have that old one in the basement.

She hurried down the rickety steps that reminded her too much of the house Flynn had taken her to. Maybe she should have Daniel fix them.

Maybe not!

With only the single bulb overhead, Rita turned on her phone flashlight as well and searched the crowded room. Momma never threw anything out. And most of this was junk. That was something a handyman could do.

Sure, he could, but only if she made that call, which she wouldn't.

She shined her light toward the corner of the room. There was the tree. It even had ornaments hanging on it. She pulled it out into the light, and screeched. And dropped it to the floor.

What she'd thought were ornaments, were thick spiderwebs. Eww. One more piece of junk. But now, what would she do about a tree? Her momma's disease would not steal Christmas celebration from her as well.

She hurried from the basement and googled Tree Farms. There were several in the area, but she had one problem. With her little car, that seemed to run only half the time, how would she get the tree from the farm to home?

Not really a handyman job, but Daniel would do it.

A mere two days after he'd dropped off his business card, and she was already caving in. She had to swallow her pride and give him a call. She didn't need the business card she'd torn up; his number remained in her phone. One more thing she should purge. After he helped her with the tree.

She dialed his number, half hoping he was on assignment and wouldn't answer.

"Hey there."

Oh, shoot, he did have a nice voice.

"Hi, um, can I take you up on your offer? I need to buy a Christmas tree and have no way to get it home."

"When do you need to go?"

She winced. "Right now?"

"Perfect. I'll be over in thirty minutes."

Thirty minutes? She sighed. Plenty of time to get Momma up and moving.

Two hours later, they had the tree up and decorated. Momma had even pitched in.

And Daniel left. Without accepting payment, just as he'd said. No strings were attached. But she wouldn't use him again.

Bright sunlight awoke Rita the next morning. After a number of dreary December days, sunshine was very welcome.

Humming "Jingle Bells," she slowly made her way to the kitchen for the necessary cup of coffee to make it through the day. She brought the pot to the sink to fill with water, looked outside, and her heart fell.

Yes, the sun was shining, but the reason it shone so brightly was because it was glistening off of snow. Several inches worth. Which meant she needed to get outside ASAP and shovel the city sidewalk before someone sent her a nasty note.

Without starting the coffee, she hurried to the living room, slipped on her boots, and grabbed her coat out of the closet.

"Where are you going?"

She looked back at Momma in her chair. "I have to shovel."

"No, you don't, it's already taken care of."

If only.

"Thank you, Momma, for shoveling. Maybe I'll go outside and make a snowman then."

"I never said I shoveled."

"Okay." Rita pulled on a mitten. "Then who did?"

"Daniel, of course."

Rita dropped her second mitten. She would have been less surprised if her momma had said "shovel fairies."

"Daniel?" Her voice broke a little. "You remember Daniel?"

"Of course, I do. He's the nice young man who helped with the house."

Rita closed her eyes, blocking in tears. These lucid moments occurred so rarely, she had to absorb them, commit them to memory so that in the other times, she could bring up the memory and cling to it.

"Come here." Momma waved her over and reached up, opening her arms.

She wanted a hug? Tentatively, Rita lowered herself into her mother's arms . . .

That tenderly wrapped around her. "You're a good daughter." Momma patted her back.

Closing her eyes could no longer rein in the tears. They slid over her cheeks as she returned the hug. "I love you too, Momma."

Just like that, Momma's arms jerked away, and her focus was once again on the television. But she'd given Rita a priceless gift.

She *was* loved. And no matter what Momma said going forward, her words moments ago couldn't be unsaid. She glanced outside at the sunlight gleaming off the snow, raised her hands, and whispered, "Thank you." And for several moments, basked in that warm hug from God.

Moments later, she opened her eyes and contemplated the other thing her momma had said: "Daniel shoveled."

So, did that mean that he had actually shoveled her walk? It wasn't Momma's imagination?

Rita ran to the front door and opened it. Both the city sidewalk and the house sidewalk were shoveled. The ramp as well. Samwise tried to squeeze past her as she stared. "No boy, you go out the other door." He barked and ran to the side door and wagged his tail. She let him outside, on shoveled steps, and peered over a shoveled walkway, which led to the garage and a shoveled driveaway.

When had he done this?

Should she call, thank him?

No. He might take a phone call from her as a sign that she wanted to get back together.

But, *Yes.* Showing gratitude was the polite thing to do, regardless of her feelings. And pride.

Instead, she sent him a quick text.

— Thank you for shoveling. —

Then she added.

— Momma remembered you. —

Moments later her phone pinged back.

— Thank you for that gift. —

And that was it. No more messages for the rest of the day. This businesslike relationship she could handle. As long as he had no romantic expectations.

Daniel pulled into his parents' parking lot beside the two minivans and crossover. As usual, he was the last to arrive, but today, he was on time. They weren't going to hold that over his head this Christmas. He was grumpy enough without their razzing.

He grabbed the bag of gifts, and the meat and cheese tray from his passenger seat. Cut and arranged by him, no less. His family wasn't going to give him grief about bringing potato chips today.

Goliath met him on the way to the house, but Daniel didn't feel like roughhousing.

It was Christmas Day. He was supposed to be joyful. But he just couldn't muster it.

He knocked on the front door before letting himself in. He formed a smile and shouted, "Ho Ho Ho, Merry Christmas," as he always did on this day and prepared himself to be tackled by four pretty little women.

At least they didn't disappoint him.

He sat on the floor and accepted all their squeeze hugs and listened to their animated tales about what Santa brought them this morning.

"You're early." Carrie shooed away the girls and offered him a hand up.

"Proud of me?"

"Shocked, is more like it." She picked up his meat and cheese tray. "Who'd you pay to do this?"

"Hey. I did it myself."

"Huh. What's up?" She walked in front of him to the dining room.

"Nothing's up. I just wanted to arrive in time for hot food."

"If you say so."

"Seriously?" He stopped. "Can't you just say, 'Merry Christmas' and leave it at that?"

"Someone got up on the wrong side of the bed."

"Yeah, and I'm looking at her."

He heard her sigh. Yeah, he'd sigh too if he had to listen to him.

He practically pouted through the meal and only had seconds, not thirds. He even yipped at his youngest niece for spilling her milk on his pants. If it hadn't been for dish duty, he'd leave and spare his family his Grinch-like attitude.

Dad helped him carry the dirty dishes to the kitchen. The rest of the family gathered in the living room and waited, probably impatiently, for them to finish cleaning so they could open presents.

"Want to talk about it?" Dad gave him a washed and rinsed coffee cup.

"No."

"Okay." Dad handed him plates, cups, glasses, silverware, all without saying a word.

"She still doesn't give me the time of day." He jutted a knife into the wood block.

No response from Dad.

Now Daniel knew why interrogations worked best if they just let the perp speak. He couldn't not say something. "Like you suggested, I gave her my handyman card, wrote that all services are free. So far, I've helped get her Christmas tree, changed her locks, put lights on her house, fixed her basement stairs, cleaned out the basement. There was an old artificial tree that spiders had taken over. I even brought her to church one Sunday 'cause her car wouldn't start. Gladys sat between us. I fixed the car, too."

"Is that all?"

"What do you mean, is that all?" He squeezed a coffee cup

between two hands, and it shattered.

"When you gave that 'free' card to her, did you really have no expectations?"

"Well." Daniel bent and picked up the broken pieces and dumped them into the wastebasket, then he swept up the rest all while contemplating his answer. "I meant what I said, I just hoped for a different outcome."

"What if nothing ever comes of this? What if she doesn't forgive you? What if she starts dating someone else? What if she keeps using her free handyman services card in spite of all that? Will you keep serving?"

"That's what I promised," he grumbled as he swept up the remainder of the broken pieces. "But I don't like it."

"Oh, I understand. Sometimes I wonder how God keeps loving us when most of us reject His gift, the One we're celebrating today. Even when we choose to follow Him, half the time we ignore Him or only turn to Him when we get ourselves in a mess."

Daniel flung the dish cloth over his shoulder and leaned his backside against the cupboard. "I'm a selfish idiot."

Dad laughed. "I wouldn't go that far, but I get it. You're tired of hurting. That's always the difficulty when you have a big heart. That big heart gets hurt, and it's painful. But it also heals. And it will love again."

Daniel sighed and wiped a hand over his face, hoping to hide the stupid tear. "Does Mom know you're this wise, or do you save all your talks for me?"

"Who do you think I get all my wisdom from?"

Momma was going to drive her insane!

What a way to spend Christmas Day.

With super-soapy water, Rita scrubbed the bathroom floor, the walls, the tub, the toilet. Momma had somehow wiped her poo everywhere. Had any actually landed inside the toilet? Then there was the mess she'd made of herself and her clothes.

Rita had heard from other caregivers about this stage of the disease, but she'd hoped it would never arrive. And this was only the beginning. How did anyone ever make it through this?

Numbly, she had Momma take a shower—which Momma fought—then Rita washed the clothes, praying constantly that this would be a one-time thing.

Once everything was clean, she checked on Momma. In her chair, watching her shows, oblivious to the mess she'd made. Guess that was a measure of grace, because the mother Rita had grown up with would be mortified.

Rita made a cup of coffee in her brand-new Keurig, a time-saving Christmas present for herself, then settled onto her bed to watch *White Christmas*. She needed something happy and hope-filled today.

In the middle of the "Sisters" song performed by Bing Crosby and Danny Kaye, her phone pinged.

Daniel.

– Merry Christmas –

She couldn't type the words back to him. It wasn't a merry day. Instead she texted.

– HELP! –

173

Seconds later another ping.

– Be right over –

Relief flooded her, making her want to cry. Twenty minutes later, Daniel was at her door, bearing wrapped presents and leftovers from his family Christmas. "From Mom."

She felt like crying again.

After heating up and eating the delicious beef, ham, and potatoes Daniel had brought, and after getting Momma tucked into bed, Rita finally had a moment alone with Daniel. Just his presence this evening had calmed her.

Had she judged him too harshly? After all, he had been doing his job—a tough job at that—and she was no longer worried for her safety. He had helped her out of the mess William had dragged her into, and he'd asked for nothing in return.

That was grace.

She fixed him a cup of cocoa, and herself a coffee, then settled beside him on the couch.

Just not too close.

"Now, how can I help?" He sipped his cocoa.

"Just being here helps."

"But there's more, isn't there?"

She nodded, sniffled, and shared her Christmas Day experience. "How do people do this day in and day out? I'm ready to put her in a home, but I know I shouldn't."

"There may come a time when that will be necessary. It killed my mom at first when Grandma went into the nursing home, but they could care for her so much better there."

"We're not to that point yet, but what do I do in the meantime? I can't call you every time I'm about to lose it."

"Why not?"

"Because that might happen every day." She chuckled lightly.

"You know." He pulled out his phone. "I might have an idea. Mind if I give Mom a call?"

"I'd appreciate her wisdom."

Minutes later, he handed her a note he'd jotted. "The local Dementia Caregivers chapter has volunteers who offer a respite day, one time per month. I'll contact them tomorrow to see about signing you up."

Rita blinked as she stared down at the number. "You'd do that for me?"

"Of course." He shrugged. "You deserve it."

She sniffled and rubbed her nose. Tears were not allowed, even though they wanted to sneak out. She managed to find her voice. "You have no idea what this means to me." She shifted closer to Daniel. Maybe it was time to forgive him.

But he leaped up from the couch. "Glad I could help, but work calls. I'm tailing an eighty-year-old man who's the chief thief in a tech theft ring." He chuckled. "The dude's crazy clever."

Disappointed by his actions, but not at all surprised, she walked him to the door, hoping he'd look at her like he had before Thanksgiving. But he avoided her gaze. Instead he opened the door and stepped out before looking back. "I mean it. If you need anything, call."

"I will." She planned to make full use of his Free Services card.

He took off down the sidewalk, but she couldn't let him leave like that. "Daniel!"

He spun around. "Yeah?"

"I forgive you." Just saying those words removed a weight from her shoulders.

His eyes closed, and he bowed his head. Seconds later, he

raised his head, and in the moonlight, she swore she saw tears glistening on his cheeks as he softly said, "Thank you."

She remained in the doorway and drew in a breath, afraid to hear the answer to her next question. "Will you go out with me?"

His entire face broke into a smile. "I thought you'd never ask."

Even with the cold air swooping inside the home, warmth filled her from her sock-covered toes to her blushing cheeks. Her heart scabs were finally healing. Maybe she was ready to love again.

Chapter Fourteen

Daniel whistled "Auld Lang Syne" as he entered the station. Like the rest of the force, he'd worked the last couple of days. What was it about New Years that made people go bonkers? They'd filled the jail cells with drinkers and rabble-rousers. Now today, the over-partiers were all sleeping it off.

And tonight, he was going on a date. A New Year's date, a day late, naturally. But he was ready. She wanted to be a princess? Well, he couldn't think of a better place for that to happen than the Policeman's Ball held annually the Saturday following New Year's. He'd never attended before—it was usually an event for the higher-ups to mingle with the wealthy as a fundraiser for disabled cops and fallen cops' families. He'd received a special invite for his part in taking down the Flynn Family.

He'd get to wear his dress blues, and Rita? Well, he'd find out tonight. He couldn't wait.

They wouldn't stay late. No, her chariot wouldn't turn into a pumpkin, but her volunteer from the Dementia Caregivers needed to be home by eleven.

She should be arriving at Rita's within the next hour, so Rita could go out and pamper herself. He couldn't wait to see her.

"Winter, get in here. Now."

What was up with Howard?

Daniel hustled to the chief's office, where Howard stood with Officers Steinbach and Kenyon. Fear zinged up his spine. "Did Flynn escape from jail again?" Was he heading to Rita's?

"No." Chief locked gazes with Daniel. "It's the sister this time."

"The sister? I thought she wasn't involved in the family business."

"She might not be, but it doesn't look good." Chief straightened papers on his desk. "We've been keeping an eye on her, and she didn't show up for work today. An employee said she'd been grumbling about avenging her father's death."

One of the officers cursed as Daniel shot out the door, ignoring the chief's calls to come back. He had no doubt the woman was headed for Rita's place, and he needed to beat her there.

Rita practically floated on air as she prepared for her day out. Didn't matter that Momma had another accident. Didn't matter that she was back to hating on Rita. Nope, because today Rita had a day off for pampering followed by a date with a very handsome cop. She planned to find a dress today that would leave him speechless. She giggled just thinking about it.

Samwise barked at her, tearing her from her daydream.

"Shhh." She put a finger to her lips. "You want to go outside, buddy? Momma's taking a nap, and we really don't want to wake her." Then she rubbed her hands on both sides of his face and he tried to lick her. "Uh-uh, not this time." She'd just gotten all freshened up and didn't need doggy slobber on her.

She opened the side door and he bounded out. Oh, he loved romping in the snow. How wonderful it was to have a fence, so she didn't have to worry about him. Thanks to Daniel.

Detective Cramer had told her Daniel had given far more than was required in his assignment to protect her. She was now seeing that he truly had hands of grace and that she was a very fortunate woman.

The doorbell chimed, and she looked at the time. A bit early for her volunteer, but that was okay. She was ready to go pamper herself any time. She rushed to the door and peeked through the hole. The woman's head was down, so she couldn't see the face. But by her wardrobe, she appeared to be a youngish woman. Dark hair did a pirouette from beneath her stocking cap. It all fit with the description the organization had given her, so she flung open the door.

"Hi Hannah, I am so glad you're—"

The woman pushed Rita out of the doorway, knocking her to the floor.

Only then did she see the woman's face.

Marion Flynn?

"Get up." The woman waved a gun at her. "Lock the doors. Set the alarm. I don't want anyone surprising us."

Breathing hard, Rita struggled to get off the ground, finally pushing herself to her feet. She felt her front pocket for her phone, but it wasn't there. Probably still sat on an end table by the couch. If, somehow, she could get it without Marion noticing . . .

"Hurry up."

Rita felt something jab her in the back, so she hurried to lock both doors and set the alarm. Why had she made Daniel change the locks and the alarm code?

"Now go sit on your couch."

She sat and saw her phone just to her left. How could she reach it with Marion watching every move? Rita had to think of some distraction.

"What do you want?" Rita said with as much calm as she could gather, which wasn't much.

The woman thrust the gun toward her. "I want you to feel what I've felt this last month mourning my father. What I felt when I learned that you were responsible for his death."

"I wasn't—"

"I didn't give you permission to talk." The woman turned to look out the window.

And Rita reached for her phone.

"Oh, no you don't." Marion grabbed it away. She had Rita turn around and put her arms behind her back.

She felt something hard wrenching her wrists together. Marion then tightened zip ties around Rita's ankles. "It was so nice of you to let your dog outside before I got here. I don't like hurting animals. Cops, though, they deserve what they get, and I do expect your boyfriend to come to the rescue."

Rita's blood froze at the realization. Marion wasn't here just to hurt Rita, she wanted to harm Daniel as well. "No doubt word has spread of my bakery not opening this morning, and what cop doesn't want to be a hero in his lover's eyes?"

"We—"

"Can it." She paced the room, her gaze moving from Rita to the front window to the side door. "Now we wait."

"It won't just be Daniel."

She shrugged. "I've got a few tricks up my sleeve."

"You're not going to hurt Daniel."

"Like you didn't hurt my father? You owe me and William. Though I'm not too happy with big brother for getting caught again. He wasn't this sloppy until you. Don't know what kind of spell you put on men. I don't get it."

The woman checked her watch and went to the front window. Then to the side door by the kitchen, then to the kitchen window and back to the living room. "Huh. Maybe lover boy doesn't care as much for you as you believe he does."

"Drop your gun."

A grin spread across Marion's face as she turned toward the basement door, where Daniel stood, his feet apart and gun trained on Marion.

"Clever." She fixed her gun on Rita and took a tiny step toward her.

"Stop," Daniel commanded, then his voice softened. "You don't want to do this, Marion. You've kept your life clean. Why ruin that? Give yourself up now and we'll make sure the courts are lenient."

"Trying psychology? Oh, believe me, Papa taught me all your tricks."

"What's going on?"

Oh, Momma.

Momma stepped right between Marion and Daniel. "I don't allow guns in this house." She looked to Daniel. "You know better than that."

"Gladys." Daniel nodded toward the hallway. "You're not ready for our date."

Momma gasped. "Oh, my, you're right."

"Stop!" Marion aimed the gun at Gladys and looked to Rita. "Get your stupid mother to sit down, or I'll put her down permanently."

"How dare you talk—"

"Momma!" Rita wished she could take her momma's hand,

keep her calm. "Your stories are on now. Come sit."

"Oh, they are?" Momma waddled to the living room toward her chair.

"Not there." Marion nodded to the couch.

"Sit by me, Momma, and share some cookies."

Rita looked toward Daniel for help. Where had he gone?

There, out of the corner of her eye. With Momma's distraction, he'd crossed to the other side of the room, closer to the front door, getting herself and Momma out of the line of fire.

"The place is surrounded, Marion." He said with far more calm than she felt. "Put your gun down. No one has to get hurt."

"Oh, but yes they do." Marion's grip tightened on the gun. "Someone has to pay for killing Father."

"Then look to your brother." Daniel moved more, so that now Marion was in between the side door and him. "He pulled the trigger."

"William wouldn't do that!"

"Are you certain?"

For the first time since she'd shoved her way in, Marion's confidence seemed to waver, and the gun trembled in her hands. "Of course, I am."

"He wanted out of the life. Your father gave him no respect."

"If he would have done his job right, Father would have respected him." A sheen of sweat broke out on Marion's face, and she rubbed it with her free arm. "You're just trying to distract me."

"Yes, I am." He grinned. "Samwise, grab!"

In a flash, Samwise knocked Marion face first to the floor. Her weapon skittered across the room.

Rita screamed.

Marion tried to rise, but Samwise growled from deep in his

throat, raising the hair on Rita's arms.

"Don't move," Daniel commanded then he stooped down and bound Marion's wrists and ankles with zip ties he'd pulled from a pocket.

Rita remained on the couch, shaking, as Daniel knelt in front of her.

"Are you okay?" Using a jackknife, he sawed off the zip tie around her ankles.

And suddenly the room filled with other cops.

She shrieked again.

"Why are all these people in my house?" Momma got up. "I need to make coffee and cookies for everyone." She shuffled toward the kitchen.

"I'm okay now." Rita concentrated on slowing her erratic breathing. She'd be even better when she could hug and kiss him. With her legs free, she stood, and he freed her hands, which she immediately wrapped around Daniel's neck.

"Not now." Daniel said softly, but firmly.

"Ah, give the woman a kiss." Detective Cramer came out of the kitchen with a peanut butter cookie as Marion was pushed out the front door. "You've both earned it."

"Because you guys took forever to get here." Daniel looked over Rita's shoulder at Howard.

"Well, when you take off half-cocked from the police station—"

"Boys." Rita looked into Daniel's sparkling blue eyes. "For once, I'd say Daniel was right on time."

She kissed him soundly, in front of his brothers in blue, who hooted and clapped and whistled.

She didn't care. And by the kiss Daniel returned, he was perfectly fine with it as well.

Epilogue

Rita twirled in the long red sequined dress she'd found at a thrift shop earlier in the day. Her hair stylist had threaded her ruby strands perfectly through her updo. She couldn't wait to see Daniel's reaction.

Four days after Valentine's Day, and he was at last taking Rita out on their Valentine's date. To a ball, at that. A fundraiser in the Twin Cities for dementia research funding. She was finally getting to be a princess.

She couldn't wait to see her handsome prince, who'd promised to wear a tux for the evening. Getting ready could take him awhile, so she'd forgive him for being late. This time.

The doorbell chimed only ten minutes after the time he'd promised to arrive, which meant he was actually twenty minutes early. She'd finally gotten smart and started telling him a time that was thirty minutes early. He'd catch on soon.

She practically floated to the door, past her momma seated in her favorite chair, watching some corny, modern-day romance while munching on popcorn. The volunteer caregiver seemed to be enjoying the movie as much as Momma.

Rita flung open the door and her breath caught.

Oh. My.

To say that Daniel looked hot in a tux, with a red tie of course, was an understatement.

"You look amazing." He circled his finger, and she twirled around, the skirt flowing out around her. He whistled. "We are going to be the best-looking couple there tonight."

She pressed her hands to his chest and looked up into his eyes. "I have no doubt." She raised on her tippy toes for a kiss.

"Well, are you going to propose, or not?" said Momma.

What?

Rita fell back on her stiletto heels and tottered.

His hands on her back steadied her.

"Well, are you, or are you not?"

Daniel adjusted his tie. "Well, I . . . "

"Come on, get it over with, so I can watch my story."

"You weren't supposed to say anything, Gladys."

"You told her you were going to propose?" Rita backed up and wrinkled her nose at him.

"I didn't think she'd remember." He fiddled with his tie some more. "And I definitely wasn't going to propose here."

She pulled his hands from his tie. "I think this is the perfect place. We have witnesses, so you can't back out."

"I, uh." He sighed. "This wasn't how I'd planned." He pulled a box from his pocket and began to get down on one knee.

Momma was right!

Oh. My. Goodness.

He opened the jewelry box displaying an oval-shaped ruby imbedded in rose gold, and held it up to her. "I know this is fast, but when you find the right person, why wait?" His head dropped. "I'm messing this all up. I had this big spiel planned, and then I see you, and my brain goes haywire." He took her hand. "But that's what you do to me. You make me smile, all the time. I adore how you love on your momma. I love your determination, your unique style, even when you want to annoy me with Pop Rocks, and for putting up with me being late all the time."

She laughed at that.

"And you look pretty amazing in red."

"Come on, come on," Momma whined. "I don't have all night. My next story is going to start."

"Guess that's my signal." He removed the ring from the box and slid it onto her finger. "Rita, will you please marry me?"

"She says yes. Now go."

"Momma!" Rita made an angry face at her momma, then turned back to Daniel. "You're going to have to put up with her as well as me. And in this house."

"I can make it bigger. Add another story with lots of bedrooms for all our kids."

She snorted. "Two. We can have two kids. No more."

He showed his lopsided grin. "Does that mean 'Yes'?"

She waggled her finger upward, getting him to stand. Then she took him by the hands that had graced her with far more love that she deserved, but that was the point of grace, wasn't it?

"That doesn't mean 'yes,' but this does." She wrapped her arms around his neck, raised up on her toes, and kissed him until her toes ached, then she captured his gaze. "Only if you promise me a whole bunch more of that." She drew her finger across his lips, now shaded in red.

"Oh, that's a promise I'll have no trouble keeping."

And he kissed her again, proving his point.

Dear Reader,

Rita and Daniel's story is a very personal one to me. When I began penning this story, I knew I needed a reason to keep Rita in her home, and the idea that kept popping up was giving her mom dementia. As my husband was recently diagnosed with early-onset Alzheimer's, I resisted this idea, but God kept nudging, and I finally gave in.

Unfortunately, dementia isn't unfamiliar to me beyond my husband. My mom had it, as did my father-in-law, and several of my grandparents. With each person, the disease looks different. Gladys's character is comprised of bits and pieces of those I've loved, along with several made-up elements that ring true with the disease.

One of the things all those I loved had in common was that they were surrounded by family who loved them, people who became hands of grace in caring for their loved ones. It's my hope that I've honored caregivers with this story, and that it encouraged you in your own personal walk with the Lord.

You'll find further inspiration and encouragement on The Potter's House Books Website, (www.pottershousebooks.com) and by reading the other books in the series. Read them all and be encouraged and uplifted!

In Him,

Brenda

Find all the books on
The Potter's House Books website.

Other Potter's House Books

By Brenda S. Anderson

Long Way Home
Place Called Home
Home Another Way

Find all the Potter's House Books at:

http://pottershousebooks.com/our-books/

Find all of Brenda S. Anderson's books at:

www.BrendaAndersonBooks.com/books

Acknowledgements

Thank you to the seven other Potter's House Books (Two) authors who are sharing beautiful stories of God molding people's lives. It's a privilege writing alongside all of you!

Thanks also goes to:

My Book Booster Team ~ for tirelessly spreading the word about my books!

Joseph Courtemanche ~ for answering police procedural questions. Any mistakes are my own.

Stacy Monson ~ for once again being my first reader and pointing out serious plot issues.

Lesley Ann McDaniel ~ for making my stories shine.

Gayle Balster ~ for reading an early draft and offering encouragement.

Sarah, Bryan, and Brandon ~ this new Alzheimer's adventure our family is going on isn't an easy one, but you've all shown marvelous grace with each step.

My husband, Marvin ~ Our new journey isn't one we would have chosen, but I promise to walk every step alongside you and will give thanks for each moment we're given!

And thank you, Jesus, for showing us what it truly means to be Hands of Grace.

Other Books

BY BRENDA S. ANDERSON

A BEAUTIFUL MESS
The Mosaic Collection

Can she love the child who broke up her marriage?

Nearly four years ago, Erin Belden's happy life became a shattered mess. After her husband admitted to an affair and that a child had been conceived, he left her and their young daughter for his new family. Now, she's finally ready to put the pieces of her life together. She's set to launch her own business and even thinks her heart might be open to romance— should the right man come along.

But just when everything seems to be lining up, she receives a devastating call: her ex-husband and his wife have been killed in a car accident, and Erin is listed in their will as their daughter's legal guardian.

How can she be a mother to the child—let alone love the child—who broke up her marriage? Does she have the courage to start over yet again and turn this mess into a mosaic of beauty?

A single mother's journey from bitterness to forgiveness.

About The Mosaic Collection

We are sisters, a beautiful mosaic united by the love of God through the blood of Christ.

An international group of authors releasing one book each month as we explore our theme, Family by His Design, and share stories that feature diverse, God-designed families. All are contemporary stories ranging from mystery to women's fiction, humorous fiction, and literary fiction. We hope you'll join our Mosaic family as we learn together what truly defines a family.

To keep informed about The Mosaic Collection books, subscribe to Grace & Glory, the official newsletter of The Mosaic Collection. You will receive monthly encouragement from Mosaic authors as well as timely updates about events, new releases, and giveaways.

Subscribe:
www.mosaiccollectionbooks.com/grace-glory/

Learn more about The Mosaic Collection at:
www.mosaiccollectionbooks.com/

Join our Reader Community, too!
www.facebook.com/groups/theMosaiccollection

Coming Home Series

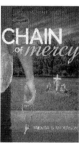

Praise for the Coming Home Series

"Anderson tackles family dynamics, tough issues, and gritty realism in her Coming Home series. From special needs babies to abortion and homelessness, you'll root for her authentic characters as they face real life struggles."

— Award-winning author, **Shannon Taylor Vannatter**

" . . . heartfelt, heart-wrenching fiction at its best, exploring relationships and family, love, faith and forgiveness in fresh, life-changing ways. I see myself in these endearing, enduring characters, their weaknesses and struggles and hard-won triumphs."

— **Laura Frantz**, author of *An Uncommon Woman*

"Anderson thrusts her readers into the gritty underbelly of family life and she doesn't mince words or shy away from the difficulties that complicate relationships. The reoccurring themes of grace and restitution are delivered with heart-wrenching honesty. These compelling stories celebrate the joys and sorrows of ordinary living with an extraordinary God."

— **Kav Rees**, BestReads-kav.blogspot.com

WHERE THE HEART IS SERIES

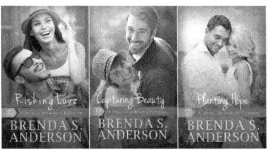

Praise for the Where the Heart Is Series

"*Risking Love* is a touching story of love and loss – and risking your heart! I can't wait to read the next in the series!"

—**Regina Rudd Merrick**, author of *Carolina Dream*

"Brenda does a great job bringing us into the story, capturing our attention and keeping it till the end. I read the first book in this series and look forward to the next. I highly recommend *Capturing Beauty* – it's an inspiring story of second chances and new perspectives!"

—**Angela D. Meyer**, author of *Where Hope Starts*

"*Planting Hope* is a lovely wrap-up to the Where the Heart Is series. The strength, or lack thereof, of a family unit has a profound impact on all of its members. Brenda Anderson expertly illustrates that in this story, and all of her books, as she deals honestly with the idiosyncrasies of families – the good, bad, and ugly. *Planting Hope* is about the hope God plants deep in our hearts, and the lengths we'll go to for those we love."

—Award-winning author, **Stacy Monson**,
author of *When Mountains Sing*

Dementia Care Resources

A number of resources are available for those on this dementia journey and their caregivers. Those that have proven invaluable to me are:

Alzheimer's Association
(https://www.alz.org/)

The 36-Hour Day: A Family Guide to Caring for People Who Have Alzheimer Disease, Other Dementias, and Memory Loss
by Nancy L. Mace, MA and Peter V. Rabins, MD, MPH

Teepa Snow: Positive Approach to Care
https://teepasnow.com/
https://www.youtube.com/user/teepasnow

About the Author

 **Brenda S. Anderson** writes gritty and authentic, life-affirming fiction. She is a member of the American Christian Fiction Writers, and is Past-President of the ACFW Minnesota chapter, MN-NICE, the 2016 ACFW Chapter of the Year. When not reading or writing, she enjoys music, theater, roller coasters, and baseball, and she loves watching movies with her family. She resides in the Minneapolis, Minnesota area with her husband of 30-plus years and one sassy cat.

Let's Connect

Visit Brenda online at www.BrendaAndersonBooks.com and on Facebook, Goodreads, Instagram, and BookBub.

For news and encouragement about upcoming books, contests, giveaways, and other activities, sign up for Brenda's bi-monthly newsletter.

If you enjoyed *Hands of Grace*, please consider leaving a review. Your words bring hope and encouragement to the author, as well as other readers.

Made in the USA
Columbia, SC
06 March 2020

88756717R00121